Praise for

BAD TASTE IN BOYS

"A dark, entertaining story." —Feathered Quill Book Reviews

"A fresh, funny, and fast-paced take on zombies
that everyone will enjoy." —booktwirps.com

"If I could sum this book up in one word,
that word would have to be awesome." —Swords for Fighting

"Be prepared to laugh. A great debut." —YA Muses

"Utterly hilarious." —Hobbitsies

"A pretty fantastic book." —sithereandread.com

"Girl + boy + zombies + betrayal = Pure win."
—wastepaperprose.com

"Brimming with laugh-out-loud moments and a lot of zombies . . .
it's one that stands out from the crowd." —stackedbooks.org

"Fun, quirky, and witty." —Cari's Book Blog

"I'm not really sure what I want more—Kate Grable as my
personal zombie protector, or my best friend—preferably both."
—The Compulsive Reader

BAD TASTE in BOYS

CARRIE HARRIS

EMBER

Text copyright © 2011 by Carrie Harris
Cover art copyright © 2011 by Emilie Brown

All rights reserved. Published in the United States by Ember, an imprint of Random House Children's Books, a division of Random House, Inc., New York.
Originally published in hardcover in the United States by Delacorte Press, an imprint of Random House Children's Books, New York, in 2011.

Ember and the E colophon are registered trademarks of Random House, Inc.

randomhouse.com/teens

Educators and librarians, for a variety of teaching tools, visit us at
randomhouse.com/teachers

The Library of Congress has cataloged the hardcover edition of this work as follows:
Harris, Carrie.
Bad taste in boys / by Carrie Harris. — 1st ed.
p. cm.
Summary: Future physician Kate Grable is horrified when her high school's football coach gives team members steroids, but the drugs turn players into zombies and Kate must find an antidote before the flesh-eating monsters get to her or her friends.
ISBN 978-0-385-73968-9 (hc) — ISBN 978-0-385-90801-6 (lib. bdg.) — ISBN 978-0-375-89806-8 (ebook)
[1. Zombies—Fiction. 2. Football—Fiction. 3. Steroids—Fiction. 4. High schools—Fiction.
5. Schools—Fiction. 6. Horror stories—Fiction.] I. Title.
PZ7.H241228Bad 2011
[Fic]—dc22
2010040027

ISBN 978-0-385-73969-6 (tr. pbk.)

RL: 5.0

Printed in the United States of America

10 9 8 7 6 5 4 3 2 1

First Ember Edition 2012

Random House Children's Books supports the First Amendment and celebrates the right to read.

ACKNOWLEDGMENTS

I am lucky to hang with some very cool people. I'd like to thank all my friends, both online and off, for making me feel cool by association. And when I said I wanted to be a writer, and you didn't laugh in my face? I really appreciated that.

I have some awesomesauce writer friends too. In particular, I need to thank Kiki Hamilton, Amy Holder, Amelia Nichols, Ellen Oh, Laura Riken, Natalie Whipple, and Kiersten White for helping make sure I don't sound like an idiot. I send you all hugs, sparkles, and ninjas with flowers.

My agent, Kate Schafer Testerman, is made of win. Thank you for sending me pictures of zombie shoes, as well as the deft-handling-of-the-business stuff and the keeping-me-relatively-sane stuff. I'm also lucky to work with some fabulous people at Delacorte Press. Thanks to the entire crew for making me feel like a rock star, and especially to my fabulous editor, Wendy Loggia, for taking a chance on my little book of zombie mayhem. My gratitude goes out to my family, particularly my mom, Mom and Dad Harris, Keith, and Sarah. Thanks for listening to me ramble on about zombies all the time and for not having me committed. Connor, Lily, and Renee, you inspired me to take a risk and follow my dreams. Thanks for putting up with all the hours I spend on the computer and for calling me over every time there's a zombie cartoon on TV. And supermegahuge thanks to Andy, fabulous husband and go-to guy for everything related to medicine, combat, and boob jokes. I wouldn't be here if it weren't for you. And yes, you told me so.

CHAPTER one

"You're one of those genius types," said Coach, nudging me with a beefy elbow. "Make yourself useful for once. Say something inspirational."

Morning football practice had just ended and I was standing in a hallway that stank of sweat and industrial cleaner, holding the door while the varsity team hauled their pitiful butts into the locker room. As the student trainer, I handled random sprains and strains, and in my spare time I pushed Gatorade like it was the nectar of the gods. But motivating the worst football team in existence? Couldn't do it.

The only thing I could think of was "Look! Naked cheerleaders!" Not exactly appropriate.

Coach elbowed me again.

"What do you want me to say?" I asked, shifting away from him. "They don't suck?"

I wasn't trying to be insulting, just honest. Earlier one of our linebackers had given himself a bloody nose by falling on his own fist, and it had gotten worse from there. Now our players looked so depressed that I thought they might commit hara-kiri.

Aaron Kingsman, the starting quarterback, trudged past. He usually nodded at me, and once he even smiled. Sad but true: that smile was the highlight of my junior year. Today he didn't even look up. He had a little cut above his right eyebrow, a bead of blood poised at one end. I wanted to give him first aid but couldn't find a way to make the offer sound reasonable. I had to say something, though.

"Nice hustle out there!" I bleated, blinking behind my glasses. They were a holdover from my formerly one-hundred-percent geeky self. Now, thanks to my friends and some expensive antifrizz conditioner, I was only fifty percent.

Aaron hunched over farther and pushed through the door.

"Way to step up, Grable." Coach made his best attempt at sarcasm. It wasn't one of his strong points. "Put this stuff away, at least, will ya?"

He handed me the keys to his office. They were on a ring the size of my steering wheel. I had no idea why one man needed so many keys. I'd counted them once: ninety-one and a half—one was broken. That key ring was heavier than I was.

Coach launched into his usual load-of-rubbish postpractice

speech before the locker room door closed, leaving me in the hallway with an entirely different load of rubbish: the Gatorade cart, clipboard, keys, and the first-aid kit. I performed my usual juggling act down the hall: push the cart two feet, drop the key ring, pick it up, lose the clipboard in the struggle, retrieve the scattered paper, push the cart another two feet, reassemble the clipboard, nearly knock the Gatorade over, and so on. On days like this, I had to chant "Kate Grable, MD" to keep from quitting. All the annoyance would be worth it when I got into a pre-med program next year.

"Kate Grable, MD. Kate Grable, *MD.*" Coach's office had one of those perennially malfunctioning fluorescent bulbs that infested our school. I didn't risk turning it on, because I was an epileptic. I hadn't had a seizure in almost a year, but before that I'd had them practically every week. It was a force of habit to avoid things that might trigger them. Flashing bulbs had always been a guaranteed ticket to seizuretown.

I propped open the door, put the clipboard on Coach's desk, and flipped through a million keys before I found the right one for the med cabinet. I had to put away Mike Luzier's EpiPen. Mike had a bee allergy and the mental capacity of a newt. We weren't supposed to leave the Epi out at night; Coach seemed to think there was a serious black-market epinephrine trade.

When I was putting the Epi in the cabinet, I noticed an unfamiliar rack of medication vials on the top shelf. The labels were blank, which instantly set off my med-geek alarm. I labeled all our drugs, and I was quite proud of my cataloging system. Even Coach could find his way around the cabinet, and he had problems following directions. Heck, he had problems reading words of more than one syllable.

I picked up the rack and a used syringe tumbled out. I yelped as the needle landed in the toe of my shoe. Carefully I extracted the needle and wrapped it in a big wad of paper towels. Coach had an ancient dispenser in his office; it squealed loud enough to raise the dead.

I wasn't sure what to make of this. Our trainer, Dr. Ho, was in charge of delivering and dispensing team meds. Everyone forgets things once in a while, but there was no way he'd leave a syringe uncapped. And Coach was the only other person with access to the med cabinet.

"Holy crap, are these steroids?" I whispered, staring down at the lump of towel in my hand. If the meds were legit, the Ho would have given me the rack for check-in. Legal drugs don't require secrecy and unmarked vials. I was pondering this when I heard the boom of the locker room door as it flew open and hit the wall.

I knew what that sound meant: Coach was coming. I slammed the office door to buy some time, vaulted the desk with more physical prowess than I knew I had, and shoved the rack back into the cabinet.

"Grable?" He knocked. "You in there?"

Duh. The door had one of those automatic locks, which meant

the desk vault had been completely unnecessary. I took a deep breath and turned the handle.

"Hey, Coach!" My voice was so perky that I wanted to punch myself.

"Grable." His eyes flicked over to the cabinet on his way in. It happened so fast I almost thought I'd imagined it.

"Clean up your crap, will ya?" he said, sitting down at his desk and scowling at the wad of paper towels. He picked it up, and I half expected him to stick himself with the needle, but apparently he was a lot luckier than I was.

"Sorry about that!" I held out my hand. "I'll throw it out for you."

He gave me an odd look before dropping it into the wastebasket at his feet. There went my evidence. I wasn't going to go Dumpster diving for it, though. Reforming geeks like me avoided Dumpsters at all costs.

I had a few minutes before first period, so I stopped by the computer lab to look up the Ho's office number. I knew he'd be at the exhibition game after school, but this couldn't wait. I found a listing for *Dr. Randy Ho—Gynecology and Acupuncture.* The thought of combining those two particular services made me want to permanently staple my knees together, but at least I was pretty sure I had the right guy. I remember Coach threw a fit when the only volunteer for the position was a "girly doctor."

I went out to the quad to make the call since it was the only place I wouldn't get lynched for using my cell. The Ho's phone rang nine times. I was just about to hang up when someone finally decided to answer.

"Dr. Ho's office," said a bored-sounding female.

"I've got an emergency. Could I talk to Dr. Ho?"

"If you have a medical emergency, you should call nine-one-one immediately."

"Not a medical emergency. An I-need-to-talk-to-Dr.-Ho-right-away emergency."

She gave me a long-suffering sigh. "What kind of emergency?"

"Uh . . ."

"Gynecology or acupuncture?"

What the heck would an acupuncture-related emergency be like? The idea was so ridiculous that I couldn't keep from snorting.

"I'm waiting," she snapped.

"Look, my name is Kate Grable. I'm the student trainer for the Bayview High football team. I need to talk to Dr. Ho. It's important."

"He's not in the office."

"Could you please let him know I need to talk to him before the exhibition game tonight?"

"If you insist, Katie." And then she hung up on me. I thought about calling her back and correcting her on the name thing but decided it wasn't worth it.

I walked out of the quad and into the hallway, which was much less crowded than usual.

"Hey, Kate! How're you?" chirped some girl I only vaguely recognized. Did I know her from Key Club? My friend Kiki had talked me into joining all kinds of social organizations, even though I hated going to meetings and could never remember anyone's name. I kept waiting for someone to realize that geeks like me didn't belong in Key Club, but it hadn't happened yet.

"I'm late," I said, waving a hand as I hurried down the hall. I was the compulsively early type, but in this case my lateness was justified. I was worried about my players collapsing on the field due to unregulated steroid use. There *was* an empty slot in the tray, not to mention the used syringe in the cabinet.

I wasn't going to let that slide.

CHAPTER two

"You'll be my lab partner today, won't you, Kate?" Kiki Carlyle asked approximately five seconds after I got the first demerit of my life for being late to AP Biology.

I used to think anyone over the age of three who went by the name Kiki deserved to be drawn and quartered with a spork. Then I got to know Kiki Carlyle, and, well—she was just about the nicest person I'd ever met. Kiki was a Triple-B: blond, busty, and brainy. She was the senior class president, head varsity cheerleader, and front-runner for salutatorian. In the halls, she said hi to everybody, even the nobodies. If she didn't have the word *perfect* tattooed on her behind, she should have.

She'd moved to Bayview halfway through freshman year, and we got assigned to the same table in earth sciences. She'd pulled me out of social purgatory, and we'd been friends ever since. We'd even stayed close when she was dating Aaron Kingsman last year. I'd been jealous, sure, but I couldn't get mad at her.

Kiki was a great lab partner. She pulled her own weight instead of expecting me to do all the work. It became even easier to work with her once she and Aaron broke up; I no longer had to feel guilty about crushing on her boyfriend. I actually wanted to be *his* lab partner, especially after he outscored me on the first bio test and left me with a B+ and the conviction that he was the most perfect guy on the planet. But it was never going to happen, because he always paired up with Mike Luzier, a total jerk who for some strange reason was his best friend.

Mrs. Mihalovic instructed everyone to gather around and watch her demonstrate the dissection process. We were doing fetal pigs. I was so excited I'd practically memorized the book. It was pretty disappointing when Mrs. M started reviewing basic dissection techniques; I wanted to start cutting so badly. But Kiki seemed content to hang in the back of the room with me. We sat at our station and didn't even pretend to listen.

"Sooo...what are you doing after the game tonight?" she asked, playing with an empty dissection tray.

That night was the annual homecoming varsity/JV game. After it was over, I planned to follow Aaron to the parking lot like the desperate semistalker I truly was. I couldn't exactly say that, though, so I fiddled with the end of my braid and shrugged.

"I'm having a bonfire, and I really think you should come," she said.

"On a school night?" I asked.

"We've got homecoming week events every other night, and my parents come back into town on Saturday. If I don't do it tonight, I can't do it at all. So what do you think?"

I sighed. "If you haven't noticed, I'm not exactly the party type." Especially after what had happened at the last party I'd gone to.

"Yeah, but Rocky will be there, and she'll be sad if you don't show. Don't you dare tell me you have to study. You could get straight As with one brain tied behind your back."

Rocky Miccuci was my best friend. On the surface, we were total opposites. She was the star of the choir . . . and I was really great at dissecting frogs. She had long curly hair that belonged in a shampoo commercial, and she liked to wear tiny dresses that would fit her five-year-old sister. She had the body for it too, unlike me, who had the body of a string bean and looked like the kind of girl who belonged in a library doing research on weird medical mysteries.

In fact, I had been that girl . . . up until last year, when I'd started branching out socially. But still.

Rocky and I had been friends since grade school, even during my übergeek years when I was last to be picked for everything there was to be picked for. She was always on me to get out and be social. "The swirlies are in the past!" she'd say. "You aren't the queen geek anymore."

Kiki was waiting for a response to her invitation, so I shrugged again.

"I'll talk to Rocky in choir," she said, giving me a smile of such brightness that I suspected my corneas might be irrevocably damaged. "We'll double-team you."

"Fine," I huffed. "I'll clear my busy social schedule if it means that much to you."

Kiki threw her arms up in triumph, knocking the dissection tray to the floor.

"Girls!" Mrs. M said, waving a small scalpel at us. "You've finished your discussion just in time."

I drove straight home after eighth period. Dad was still at work, and my mom was teaching theoretical physics for two semesters in Germany. Mom and I were supposed to Skype at three-thirty. I wanted to get back to school before Coach, though, so I nuked a plate of spaghetti before going to the computer.

I sat at my dad's desk and ate while the laptop booted up. Armstrong, our dog, stared at me with his most pitiful expression until I gave him a noodle. He loved pasta, and I was a sucker for his cute doggy face.

Mom appeared on the screen just as I shoved a huge bite into my mouth. Sauce dribbled down my chin.

"*Guten Tag!*" she said.

"Mmph!"

She laughed. "Early dinner, huh?"

"Gotta leave for the game in a half hour. It's homecoming week," I said, covering my mouth with one hand to avoid spewing tomato sauce all over the screen. "I'm sorry. I should have told you before."

"That's all right; I have about a hundred projects to grade tonight anyway. But I didn't want to miss our weekly chat." She smiled at me. "I miss you."

"Miss you too, Mom."

"So did you talk to him yet?"

About a month ago, when I was desperate for conversation material, I'd made the mistake of telling her about my crush on Aaron. And ever since, she'd been pestering me to ask him out. I could barely string together two words in his presence; something told me that wasn't going to happen.

"I'll do it, Mom. Just give me time," I said.

"You say that, but you never do it. For all you know, he really likes you."

"He barely knows I exist. And he only knows at all because I bring him Gatorade."

"He'll never know you exist if you don't talk to him."

I loved my mother, but her constant pep talks killed me. It was hard to keep the exasperation out of my voice. "I. Will."

"Tonight," she said firmly. "And I expect a full report on Sunday afternoon during family chat."

"No way. Not in front of Jonah. I'll never hear the end of it."

Jonah was my little brother. I'd have given myself a paper cut and soaked it in battery acid before I told him I liked a guy.

"Good point," she said. "Next week, then."

"All right." I took another bite. I thought about bringing up the steroids and asking for her help, but what was she going to do? She wasn't even in the country. It was my problem to deal with, whether I liked it or not.

"I'm so sorry to cut this short, honey," she said, "but I've really got to run. These papers won't grade themselves."

"Love you, Mom."

"Love you too."

I signed off and shoveled down the rest of my food. Then it was time to go back to school for the game.

Time to get my hands on one of those vials.

"You're the varsity!" screamed Coach, his forehead bulging. "They're the JV! You should win this, you sissies! I don't care if this is an exhibition game; I just want you to score one freaking touchdown for a change!"

The night was not going well. I hadn't been able to get into Coach's office; he'd spent the entire afternoon blabbing on his office phone with his feet up on the desk, and I thought he might notice if I took some of the black-market drugs out of the cabinet right next to him.

The Ho hadn't shown up, so the team went onto the field

without him. I'd set up my kit on the sidelines, totally distracted because Aaron was warming up about ten feet away. He noticed me watching him and did his little nod thing in my direction. Every cell in my body squeed in unison.

Coach started screaming as soon as the teams lined up for the first play. It looked almost comical; on average, our varsity players had two years and about fifty pounds on the JV guys. But I still wasn't surprised when the whistle blew and the JV overran our team like a herd of Pamplona bulls. Blocking had never been our strong suit. They hit Aaron really hard; I heard the *whoosh!* his lungs made when all the air was forced out. I wanted to beat the heck out of the JV guys for that, except I wouldn't know what to do in a fistfight without a manual.

"Get up," I urged from my spot on the sidelines, clenching my fists so hard that I could feel my nails dig into my palms. "Come on. Get up."

He staggered to his feet. I had to resist the urge to cheer as he straightened his helmet. The players lined up again, Aaron calling out numbers that sounded completely random to me. Derek LaBianca snapped him the ball, and the JV team took him down again before he could get rid of it.

With two minutes left in the half, the ball squirted out of Logan Smith's hands, and every single guy on the field leapt at it. I shifted nervously as the refs began pulling padded guys off the mound of players and didn't relax until I saw Aaron's face. He wasn't hurt, and he even had the ball.

But after everyone else got up, Logan was still rolling around in the grass, clutching his hand. Coach didn't ask if Logan was okay. Instead, he charged out onto the field and started yelling. I barely registered the words at first; I was too busy staring at Coach's face. He'd been chewing ferociously on a pen, and his lips were stained with blue ink.

"Jeez, Smith!" Coach ranted. "You look like one of Jerry's Kids! What do you mean you got to sit out on the next play? Man up and get back in the game."

No one intervened, not even the referees. We sucked so badly that the officials didn't even pay any attention. No one in the bleachers cared either; the only reason anyone showed was because the Key Club was giving out free Lady Gaga bobble heads at halftime. Normally, about five people came to our games, and two of them ran the concession stand.

I walked across the field to stand behind Coach.

"Excuse me?" I said, tugging on his sleeve. "I've got to clear him to play."

He whirled, flinging blue-tinged spittle into my eye. The guy was practically foaming at the mouth. "Grable. What do you want?"

"He's not allowed to play until someone checks him out."

I met his gaze without faltering, even though my eyes wouldn't stop watering from the spit projectile. Coach got right up in my face and smiled so wide I could see every single one of his teeth. With the blue lips, he looked like an apoplectic clown. I hated clowns.

"Of course, Grable. I'll just let you handle it." He rubbed his forearm like there was an itch he knew he shouldn't scratch but couldn't help himself. "I'll let you handle it all."

I actually liked it better when he was yelling; the unhinged smile was way too borderline psychotic for my taste. But poor Logan still stood there, cradling his pinky and looking humiliated, and he deserved my undivided attention. It seemed like a simple fracture, but I took him to the EMT station at the end of the field just to make sure. I loved it when the EMTs agreed with me. And they did. They even let me splint it.

I returned to the sidelines as the halftime buzzer sounded, and we made the March of Shame back to the locker room. I never bothered to follow the score, but I knew it was something along the lines of a bunch of points for them and no points whatsoever for us.

Things didn't go according to the standard protocol after that. Usually, Coach followed the team into the locker room, but this time he pulled Aaron out of line, whispered to him, sent him in, and stayed behind.

"Grable," said Coach, gesturing to me. "My office."

I was more curious than anything else, because I couldn't see him finding fault with anything I'd done. He had to concede that I was right about Logan; I'd gotten him off the field efficiently and back in working order as soon as possible. What more did he want? If he asked me to shout encouragement at the players again, I was going to encourage him to stuff it up his behind.

I followed him down the hall and let him fumble with the keys for once. It gave me time to ponder his last name, which was printed on a nameplate on the door and contained enough Zs to require three sets of Scrabble tiles to spell. Which would explain why everyone just called him Coach.

He turned on the light and held the door for me in a rare gentlemanly gesture. When I walked into the office, the rack of vials sat right in the middle of his desk.

I didn't know how to react. Somehow, gaping seemed insufficient, but I still did it.

"You need to do something for me, Grable," said Coach, sitting down and pointing me toward a rickety folding chair.

"What's that?" I sat gingerly, tearing my eyes away from the vials. Maybe I was wrong. Maybe they were B12.

"Ho is delivering a baby." Coach set a box of syringes atop the vials and pushed the stack toward me. "He was supposed to administer these tonight. Since he's not here, you need to do it."

"What's in the vials?"

"That's not your concern."

"Of course it is, if you want me to administer them."

"Fine. They're B twelve."

"Why aren't they labeled?"

"You ask too many questions, Grable. Just do what you're told."

"Excuse me?" I shoved the rack back toward him and jumped to my feet. "You're never supposed to administer medications from unlabeled containers. And anyway, I'm just a student trainer.

I'm not supposed to give injections. We both know that, so don't order me around like I'm an imbecile."

He just scowled at me. Like that was going to change anything.

"If you don't have anything legal you'd like me to do, I'd like to check on Smith's pinky."

"Get out," he said.

I didn't need to be told twice.

I wanted to call Rocky and rant for a while, but I needed to check on Logan. We were low on players. Five guys were out sick, one had a strained groin, two had sprained their ankles at practice that morning, and Joe Wisniewski got a nosebleed if you looked at him funny.

I took a deep breath before tapping on the locker room door. After a minute, Aaron stuck his head out.

"What's up?" He looked at me a little closer. "Something wrong?"

I was still angry, but I didn't want him to think of me as a hostile person. I took another breath and spoke as calmly as possible. "Can you send Logan out so I can take a look at his finger?"

"No problem. Are you sure there's nothing wrong, Kate?"

It was the first time he had ever said my name. All the anger rushed out of me. I felt drained and breathless, like I'd just run a mile, and my heart started beating double-time. I couldn't form any words, so I just nodded.

"By the way, you're doing a great job out there," he said, leaning on the doorframe and smiling at me. "I've been watching."

"No wonder you keep getting clobbered. Quit doing that."

I couldn't believe I said that. Well, I could, but I didn't want to. I expected him to slam the door in my face, but he laughed instead. I wasn't sure if he thought I was joking or was just too polite to point out what a moron I was.

"Trust me," he said before closing the door, "during a play, all I'm thinking about is not getting clobbered. I'll send Logan out."

I'd just engaged in witty banter—how in the heck had that happened? Maybe I wasn't as hopeless as I thought. My mother would never let me live this down.

I kept replaying it in my head: the way he laughed at my joke, the way he looked at me like I was interesting and not just like he wanted to copy off my test. The situation had me all in a tizzy.

Logan came out the door, and I grinned like a complete lunatic. He stared at me like I'd grown a third eye.

"What?" I asked.

"I don't think I've ever seen you smile. What's up?"

"Oh. Nothing." I beamed at him. "How's the finger?"

"Hurts." He held his hand out. The tape was slipping, so we sat down next to the cart to repply it. My hands started sweating about halfway through. The elation quickly wore off and was replaced with a feeling of dread. Would Aaron expect me to flirt like that again? What would I say? Something told me he wouldn't be interested in hearing random factoids about fungal infections.

Now I was so worked up that I couldn't stop shaking. I whacked Logan's injured finger against my thigh by mistake. His face went white, but he didn't say a word.

"I am so sorry," I said, wiping my hands on my pants. "Are you okay? Do you need painkillers? Ice? Gatorade?"

"It's okay." He stood up. "I think that'll get me through the game. Thanks, Kate. You've been really great."

"You're welcome."

I felt so ashamed. It was a minor miracle that I had managed to talk to a guy without making a total fool of myself, but I needed to chill. I had a job to do, after all.

It was time to get back on the field. I reluctantly tapped on Coach's door.

"What?" he yelled.

"Time to go back out, Coach."

He opened the door. "How's the finger?"

He had a tray of steroids in his office. Was he seriously worried about a broken finger?

"Fine," I said, and then I turned my back on him and walked away before I said something I'd regret.

Not that I was going to let the steroid thing slide. No way. I actually felt a little protective now. Steroids could kill, and I wasn't about to let that happen to any of my players.

CHAPTER three

After the game, my brother, Jonah, met me outside the locker room wearing a giant chicken suit. Every year, a freshman was chosen to be our team mascot, Birdy the Bantam. The costume had to be one of the most emasculating things in the known universe, particularly since Birdy was a girl and wore a cute little cheerleading outfit complete with yellow tights and pigtails.

Jonah wasn't usually the school-spirit type, but he had an epic crush on Kiki. Being our mascot allowed him to spend a lot of time on the sidelines ogling her and the other cheerleaders. I tried to tell him Kiki wasn't attracted to giant cheerleading chickens, but he never listened to me.

"Take me with you," he squeaked. I thought he might finally be hitting puberty. He was fifteen, so it was about time.

"What on earth are you talking about?"

He shadowed me to Coach's office. "You've got to let me come with you to Kiki's bonfire."

"I don't think cheerleading poultry are allowed. Besides, I'm only staying for a minute to be polite, and then I'm going home."

"Please. Please, Kate." He patted my arm desperately with his wings, trying to grab me, but the costume had no hands. "I swear; I'll do anything. I'll do all your chores for a month."

He sounded so desperate that I figured I might as well take pity on him; it wasn't like I'd be there long enough for him to embarrass me anyway.

I sighed. "Fine. Just get out of my way so I can lock this stuff up."

He obediently flattened himself against the wall so I could push the Gatorademobile up to the office.

When I knocked, Coach yelled through the door. "I'm busy!"

I sighed again. "Jonah, can you hand me that clipboard?"

It took him three tries to pick it up due to his hand impediment. I grabbed the papers off the clipboard and shoved them under the door. They contained personal medical information, which couldn't be left in the open.

"Screw it," I said, looking over the remaining supplies on the cart. "If someone wants the Gatorade that badly, they can have it. Let's go."

Jonah squealed, jumping up and down and shaking his pom-poms. His skirt swished around his scrawny yellow knees.

"Jonah, can I give you a piece of sisterly advice?"

"Yeah."

"If you ever want to lose your virginity, don't do that again. Ever."

He dropped the pom-poms. It wasn't much of an improvement.

When we tried to pull into Kiki's driveway about an hour later, it was so jammed with cars that I had to park on the grass. Jonah bounced incessantly on the seat beside me. I already had a headache.

"We're not staying long," I warned him.

"You say that now, but maybe you'll have such an awesome time you won't want to leave," he said.

I snorted. "Yeah, that'll happen."

But I did need to be appropriately social. Aaron would be here, expecting more of my quick wit. All I had to do was be myself, minus the overly intellectual jokes and random spouts of medical trivia.

I felt sick. But if I didn't show, both Kiki and Rocky would be upset. I had to go.

As I reached for the door handle, Mike Luzier vaulted out of the bushes, slammed against the side of my car . . . and vomited profusely all over the hood. The mess splattered with a disgusting wet noise, spraying all the way across the car and dripping off the other side. The vomit was black and viscous, and I could smell it from inside the car with the door closed. It smelled like toasted crap.

"Nasty!" Jonah squealed.

"You're cleaning that up," I said, without missing a beat.

"No way."

"Clean it up or I'll have to go home right now and do it myself. And I'll take you with me. No Kiki stalking for you."

"Come on! That's totally unfair."

"You promised to do all my chores if I brought you with me," I said. "Your first chore is to clean off the car."

I tossed a box of antibacterial wipes into his lap and got out before he could object. Mike was standing next to the hood, wiping his chin. He looked much less dazed than one would expect, given the gymnastic regurgitory display he'd just put on. I wondered what god-awful substance he'd been drinking and why he wasn't flat on his back.

He mistook my scientific observation for something else. "Couldn't wait for a repeat, huh?" he said, leering and breathing puke fumes right in my face. Then he looked around to make sure no one was watching and grabbed my butt.

I was about to verbally ream him, but then Rocky and Kiki came down the driveway toward us. Mike immediately released me and backed away into the shadows. Apparently I was good enough to grope, just not in public. He disappeared so fast that I almost thought I'd hallucinated the entire thing.

Then the breeze blew the smell of vomit past my nose.

What a tool.

I turned and pasted a smile on my face. "Hey, Rock. Kiki."

Midhug, Rocky looked over my shoulder at the lovely mess on my hood. "Oh my god, are you okay?"

I waved my hand dismissively. "Mike Luzier. It was a puke-and-run."

Kiki snorted, covering her mouth. "I'm sorry. I shouldn't be laughing."

"I don't mind. I'm not the one who has to clean it up," I said.

Jonah had wrapped his hand in wipes and was dabbing ineffectually at the hood. He must have been able to sense Kiki's eyes on him; he turned so red you could see it from fifty feet away.

"I'd let you wash your car, but some idiot stole our hose. I can get some old towels for you, though." Kiki started back toward the house. "And I'll bring you a drink," she called over her shoulder.

Jonah was going to pee twice and die when she delivered those towels.

"So did Mike say anything to you?" Rocky asked.

"He asked if I wanted seconds," I said.

"He did not!"

"Yep."

"And what did you say?"

"I took him up on it. Hooking up with him was the best moment of my young life. And barf really turns me on."

"You did not!"

"I'm joking, Rocky." I shook my head. "Of course I didn't. I wish I hadn't done it the first time."

"Well, you did," she started, but then Kiki walked back down the driveway juggling a stack of towels and a couple of plastic cups. Thank god. Rocky knew I didn't like talking about my moronic Mike moment but persisted in bringing it up anyway. I felt pretty stupid for hooking up with such a loser, even if I had been under the influence at the time. And to make matters worse, now he was convinced I was easy.

I turned away from Rocky, hoping she'd get the point and shut up about it already.

"Somebody take one of these cups before I spill all over the place," said Kiki, walking carefully over to us.

"I don't think you want that stuff on your towels, Kiki," I said, taking the cups. "It really reeks."

"They're destined for the garbage bin anyway. Be right back."

I thought Jonah really was going to pee when he saw Kiki walking toward him. He managed to trip over his own foot instead. He put a hand out to steady himself—right in the middle of the black glop on my hood—and shrieked like a little girl. I couldn't exactly blame him. I had a good stomach for that sort of thing, but it still grossed me out. Kiki held out a towel and murmured something soothing as she helped him clean up. I couldn't watch anymore; he was practically panting.

Rocky took her cup and gulped down half of its contents. I stared at mine. I didn't even like beer. Parties were so not my thing. I wondered if it was too early to leave.

"Kate!"

Aaron sprinted toward us, shouting my name. Maybe parties *were* my thing. I wasn't sure whether to be excited or frightened.

"Uh . . . yeah?" I dropped the beer out of sheer nervousness. It sprayed foam all over my shoes. Brilliant, Kate. Just brilliant.

"We need you," he said, grabbing my hand. "Medical emergency."

And then I was running through the yard hand in hand with Aaron. It was very romantic except for the part where I yelled, "Rocky, get the first-aid kit out of my car! And make sure you don't get any puke on it!"

CHAPTER four

I spent the first minute of our sprint trying not to squeal in Aaron-induced excitement and the next minute trying not to trip over anything. Then it occurred to me that I was hurtling toward a medical emergency. It would be smart to gather a little more intel before we got there and I actually had to do something useful.

"What happened?" I gasped. I was not the running type. Aaron was doing most of the work and dragging me along behind him.

"We were standing by the fire, and he just collapsed. I didn't know what to do, so I came looking for you."

"Who?" I asked, but it was barely audible. Not enough airflow to my lungs. So it was no surprise when he didn't respond.

Aaron led me across an expanse of manicured landscape and into a barren field behind the house. The bonfire loomed in the middle, stacked high with wooden pallets and shooting sparks into the air. The space was ringed with lawn chairs and packed with people who should have been busily making fools of themselves but instead were standing in a silent, sober cluster.

I'd been out in the semidark for too long; the light from the fire completely blinded me. Little red splotches danced across my field of vision. I managed to dodge the black shadowy things that I was pretty sure were my classmates but promptly tripped over a prostrate figure at my feet.

The moment I looked down, I knew something was very, very wrong.

It was Mike. His entire body was bent backward in an unnatural arc; his hands were curled into stiff and unmoving claws. His eyes bulged from their sockets. His face was a rictus mask, his mouth a frozen, leering grin.

He was dead.

A dead body was definitely more than I was prepared for. I stood there and gaped until Rocky and Kiki ran up with my first-aid kit.

"What do you want us to do?" said Kiki, panting.

The complete confidence in her voice snapped me out of it, and I started moving. It was all gloriously instinctual once I got started. Or it would have been glorious if not for the dead guy.

"Kiki, I need crowd control," I said. "Keep them back so I have room to work."

Before I even finished speaking, she was on the move. The crowd parted for her like the Red Sea for Moses, and she started to herd them like sheep. I couldn't remember if Moses was a shepherd or not, but I was under a lot of pressure, so I felt entitled to a mixed metaphor.

"Rocky, my kit, please," I said.

She set it on the ground in front of me before I even finished the sentence.

"Did anyone call nine-one-one?" I asked, snapping on a rubber glove.

No response; I looked up at a bunch of blank, wide-eyed faces. Now they really did remind me of sheep, the way they were milling about aimlessly, useless under pressure. Maybe Mike wouldn't be dead if they weren't so sheeplike. Someone could have done something to help him instead of standing around and waiting for the Kate cavalry.

"I don't think so," said Aaron, pulling out his cell.

I put my nongloved hand on his wrist to stop him. "No, I need you to tell me exactly what happened. Rocky, you call."

She nodded and took a couple of steps back, whipping out her phone. I reached down to feel for Mike's pulse with my gloved hand. The glove might have been overkill, but I had no idea what was wrong with him. I didn't know if it was contagious.

"I already told you what happened." Aaron knelt beside me and let out a strangled whimper. "He's dead, isn't he?"

I couldn't feel a pulse. I didn't think CPR would help, but if I didn't at least try, I'd always wonder if I gave up too soon. No way I could live with that.

I was so glad I'd asked for a CPR mask for Christmas; I popped it into shape and held it out to Aaron.

"I need you to do this for me," I said.

"But isn't he dead?" Aaron looked at me desperately, wanting reassurance I couldn't give. His bare arm brushed mine. It was like an electric shock; even my toes tingled. What kind of pervert gets all worked up in the presence of a corpse? I was pretty sure I needed therapy.

I shook my head and tried to focus. "We've got to try. Put the mask over his mouth and nose." I thrust it at him insistently. "Hold it tight against his face so it seals. When I say, give two breaths through the valve. I compress; you breathe. You got that?"

He stared at the mask.

"Take it!" I snapped, and this time he listened.

He couldn't get the mask to seal. Mike's face was too contorted, his teeth bared and jaw stretched wide. The expression freaked me out. I tried to close his mouth, but it was like trying to move a marble statue.

I knew rigor shouldn't set in that quickly. I tried to push his hands out of the way to do the compressions, but they were frozen in place too. The only way I'd move him was by breaking his bones.

I heard a siren in the distance. It was the most beautiful sound I'd ever heard. Best of all, now I had something to listen to other than my idiot classmates. Kiki was doing a great job of keeping them out of my way; too bad they wouldn't shut up.

"Oh my god!" said a girl to my right.

"Is he dead?" asked another.

"What are you doing, Caden?" A shocked voice from the left.

"Video, dude. This is going up on YouTube."

"That's so tactless."

I blocked out the commentary and tried the mask again. And again. I would not give up until someone pronounced Mike dead; then I would go somewhere and cry, and then I would vow not to attend another party for the rest of my life.

I have some very bad history with parties and Mike Luzier. The first time Kiki talked me into going to a party, I drank one too many glasses of "punch" and decided it would be a good idea to hook up with him. At the second one he up and died. It was quite apparent that I was not meant to go to parties. Or to be anywhere near Mike Luzier.

I tried shoving the mask on this time, as if brute force ever solved anything. I was so determined to make the stupid thing work that it took me a minute to realize Aaron was shaking me. I'd actually forgotten he was there.

"Kate?" He pointed at Mike's arm. "What is that?"

I didn't see anything at first, not until Aaron grabbed Mike's arm and showed me the black dot on his tricep. It was surrounded by a halo of greenish-yellow flesh.

I instantly knew what it was. An injection site.

Before I could say anything, two paramedics sprinted into the backyard.

"Dude, over here!" someone yelled.

They ran toward us. I stood and was just about to brief them on the situation when Mike sat up and, for the second time that night, groped my butt.

I couldn't help it. I screamed.

CHAPTER five

The EMTs looked back and forth between Mike and me, trying to determine whether they ought to be treating the butt groper or the screaming hysteric. Mike got to his feet with a noise somewhere between an exhalation and a moan and threw the CPR mask at me. It bounced off my forehead with a hollow *pock* and spiraled into the fire.

Everyone except Aaron started applauding. Mike didn't clap either; he was too busy staring at his hand like he was wondering what it was and if he could eat it. His skin looked gray in the firelight. It was an improvement over the psychotic death grin of a minute ago, but not by much.

"Water," Mike mumbled, shambling toward the house.

The EMTs finally did something useful. One intercepted Mike at the back door, and the other came over to talk to us.

"Good work," the EMT said.

"Excuse me?" I took off my glove and threw it into the fire. I kept expecting the adrenaline to hit, but I just felt numb.

"Looks like you did the job for us, Ms. . . . ?"

"Grable. Kate Grable."

"Gotcha. Well, we'll check him out, but I imagine it's just another case of alcohol poisoning. Was he drinking?"

"I, um, don't know. I just got here."

Normally, I would have been bouncing at the chance to brief an EMT on a medical emergency, but not after what had just happened. I couldn't believe Mike had walked away. Not after what I'd seen. Dead people don't get up all of a sudden. How could I have been so wrong?

"We'll give the guy a once-over just in case," the EMT said. "Thanks again, Kate. You ought to consider a career in the medical profession."

I ought to consider a lobotomy if I couldn't even tell if someone was dead or not.

Rocky escorted me into the living room, where I let myself fall onto a leather couch that probably cost the national budget of some small island nation. Maybe that was where I should go to practice medicine. Places like that were so starved for medical assistance, they wouldn't mind if I was a complete hack.

She sat down beside me. "Kate?"

"Yeah." I covered my face with a pillow. I wanted to die.

"What's—" She stopped, and then in a completely different tone of voice, said, "Do you think he should be doing that?"

I inched the pillow away from my eyes. Rocky pointed through a set of French doors toward the dining room, where one of the EMTs was smacking some kind of fancy medical scope like he thought that might miraculously make it work. Then he tossed it into his kit and kicked that closed. You aren't exactly supposed to throw those things around. Even I knew that, and I was a complete idiot.

"No. He shouldn't." I buried my face.

"Uh, Kate? What's wrong?" Rocky asked.

"I'm mentally defective."

"You saved Mike's life!"

I lowered the pillow. "I thought he was dead, Rocky. And what's worse? Even though I thought that, I still got a thrill out of rubbing arms with Aaron."

He walked in with a glass of water just in time to hear that. I really wanted to die now.

"Drink this," he said, like I hadn't just made a total fool of myself.

I covered my furiously red face again. "I don't want it. Thanks."

Aaron took the pillow away. It was really tempting to hide behind my hands, but that was a little too immature even for me.

"Look," he said, setting the pillow on the floor. "My best friend just collapsed, and I could tell by the look on your face that you recognized the mark on his arm. You're smarter than all of us put together. Help me figure out what just happened. Please?"

I gazed at the little cut above his eyebrow. And then I told him everything I knew about the vials.

"It could be nothing, but it seems like a tremendously big coincidence to me," I finished, hoping I came off as semirational.

"I don't believe in coincidences," Aaron said.

"Me either," I replied, trying not to sound as relieved as I felt. He didn't think I was nuts. "And Coach locked himself in his office after the game. He was probably getting the steroids. Maybe Mike's allergic to them."

"Or they're contaminated," Aaron said. "They're not exactly regulated by the FDA."

"Okay. So we have a possible explanation, but what about opportunity? Were you with Mike all night? Did Coach have the opportunity to give him the drugs?"

"Yeah, he did." Aaron ran his fingers through his hair. "He met with each of the players after the game. One by one, in his office. It took forever."

"Really? What for?"

"He said he wanted to give us individual feedback, but all he told me was not to get tackled so much." Aaron frowned. "As if I needed someone to tell me that. Honestly, the whole thing seemed pretty strange to me."

We were sitting with our heads close together, practically

whispering. If I had a diary, I'd write all about this later and probably dot all my *is* with little hearts out of sheer romantic starvation.

It was a good thing I didn't have a diary.

Rocky spoke up. "Uh, guys?"

I jumped. I'd forgotten she was there.

"Aren't you overlooking something?" she said. "If Coach was going to give somebody steroids, wouldn't he dose the quarterback first? I mean, that's what I'd do if I wanted to win."

"Maybe he wanted to test it first," I said. "Like, he gave them to a couple of guys to see how they'd react before doing the whole team? Or maybe he knew Aaron would say no, and he picked the guys he thought would be least likely to ask questions."

"That's true." Aaron looked kind of embarrassed, but he smiled at me anyway. "I may suck, but at least I suck honestly."

"You're assuming that Coach is the one who shot him up," Rocky said. "Maybe Mike's taking them on his own."

"Nah." Aaron shook his head. "Mike can be a moron sometimes, but he's a good guy once you get to know him. And he's no user. I'll ask him what happened, and I'll see what I can learn from the other guys while I'm at it. If Coach gave them something, they'll tell me."

"I'll check in with Kiki to make sure no one else has been sick tonight," Rocky said.

They stood up and looked at me like they were waiting for me to add something brilliant. "I'll stay here, if that's okay with you guys," I said.

"You sure you're okay?" Aaron asked, patting my arm.

I nodded. I just needed a minute to chill. It was too much to handle: Mike's collapse, the CPR, the steroids ... not to mention the fact that Aaron had spoken more words to me today than in the last three years combined. I knew, because I'd counted.

Maybe I should have felt guilty about not helping them, but I'd already done my part. True, my part had consisted of fiddling with the CPR mask, but still. I'd done it. Besides, I was afraid I'd bump into Mike if I ran around investigating, and he was the last person in the world I wanted to see.

Unfortunately for me? He walked into the living room five minutes after Aaron and Rocky left.

Mike stopped a few feet away, staring me down with an expression that said he was trying to figure out if I'd taste better with ketchup or mayo. I had this irrational urge to burrow into the smooth leather of the couch and pretend I didn't see him.

"Hi, Mike. Are you, um, okay?" I sat up straighter, hugging my pillow like it might offer some protection. From what, I didn't know.

He nodded slowly.

I hadn't thought it was possible for me to get more nervous, but I did. Now I couldn't stop chattering.

"Well, I'm glad to see you. You had us worried for a second, you know. Everybody, I mean. We were all pretty worried there. But the EMTs gave you a clean bill of health, huh?"

"No."

He just kept staring. I actually found myself wishing for his usual Neanderthal behavior. His fixation on me was almost pathological.

"Well then, maybe I should, uh, check you out instead. I mean, would you mind if I checked your pulse and stuff? Just in case. Not like I think there's anything wrong with you, of course, because obviously there isn't," I babbled.

He nodded again. I stood up, my heart beating erratically. The EMTs weren't going to give protected medical information to a high school student, and it looked like Mike had refused treatment anyway. If I wanted to know anything, I had to find it out for myself.

There's nothing to be afraid of. My instinct to run shrieking out of the room was ridiculous. I placed two fingers on the side of his neck. I didn't like how his skin felt, chilled and slightly stiff. Given the fact that I had thought he was in rigor about fifteen minutes ago, it wasn't entirely unexpected, but I didn't have to like it.

I couldn't find his pulse. I couldn't concentrate.

"Are you sure you're okay?" I asked nonsensically. Of course he wasn't okay. If he was, he wouldn't be staring at me like he was a lion and I was a nice juicy antelope.

I looked up at him and his face was right there, blank eyes devouring me. The corner of his mouth curled up in a smile more predatory than friendly, and he raised a hand to stroke my cheek. It was time to run away, but I froze. And then? He swooped down, pressing his cold, fishy lips to mine.

He tasted like old bile and rotten meat. I caught the faint smell of vomit, undercut with spicy cologne that only made the stench even more disgusting.

I flailed around in an attempt to break the kiss, twisting my head and shoving his chest and shoulders, but he wouldn't let me go. His hand clamped onto the back of my neck. He bit down hard on my lower lip, drawing blood. The coppery tang that flooded my mouth was actually a relief because I couldn't taste him anymore.

When he finally released me, I shrieked, "Get off!" Then I scrambled backward, stumbling over the couch and nearly falling over. There was a smear of blood on his bottom lip. He didn't even bother to wipe it away.

I fled down the hall, looking back over my shoulder. As I watched, he idly began to chew, the blank expression still on his face. Had he taken off a chunk of my lip?

I had to get out of there. But when I threw open the front door, I ran smack into Kiki.

"Listen, Kate," she said in a rapid, breathless voice that didn't sound at all like her. "You'd better clear out. I think the EMTs called the cops. I'd hate for you to get in any trouble, especially after what you did tonight."

"Uh . . ." I couldn't think straight. I couldn't get the gross taste out of my mouth. "I need Rocky."

"She's on bottle detail all the way out in the back. Did you bite your lip? You're bleeding. Like *really* bleeding. Gimme a sec. I'll get you something."

I nodded. I didn't want to talk about what had just happened. I wanted to forget it entirely, except my lip was throbbing hard enough to make that pretty much impossible. Kiki dashed into the house and ran out a moment later with a handful of tissues. I pressed them to my mouth despite the pain.

"Thanks for everything, Kate. I'm so glad you were here." She squeezed my arm. "Get home safe and get some well-deserved rest, okay?"

"But . . ."

I couldn't come up with a rational reason to stay. Besides, I couldn't stop shaking, and I really wanted to go home. I had the intense urge to brush my teeth for the next half hour or so and maybe follow that up with a nice carbonic acid gargle.

I'd just have to text Rocky. Maybe she could come over and take care of me while I had a complete meltdown.

I walked out to the car, looking over my shoulder about every five seconds. The driveway was almost empty already. Jonah sat in the passenger seat, obsessively scrubbing his hands with an antibac wipe.

"So . . . ," he said while I dug my phone out of my pocket and started tapping away at the keys. "That party sucked."

CHAPTER six

I vaulted out of the car the second we pulled into our driveway. I had to brush my teeth or I'd vomit. I used about half a tube of toothpaste, and it made my mouth sting like mad, but it made me feel a little better anyway.

I stared at myself in the bathroom mirror. "Oh my god." A chunk was missing from my lower lip. And it was oozing.

"You got a tetanus shot last summer," I told myself. "You're going to be fine." A lovely black scab was starting to form, so I wouldn't need stitches. But I could feel a wave of hysteria threatening to wash over me.

I needed Rocky.

She still hadn't texted me back, so I called her. Rocky liked to save her minutes, because she'd been racking up overage charges like crazy ever since her boyfriend had left for basic training. Her parents made her pay them, so she was trying not to use the phone too much. But this was a special situation.

It went straight to voice mail. I waited for the beep. "Call me, damn it!"

Being gnawed on had pushed me over the edge. Mike had always been a tool, but not the kind of tool who bit people when he had the munchies. I couldn't imagine a steroid that turned people into cannibals, although I vaguely remembered reading about a boxer who bit some guy's ear off, so maybe it was possible. Or maybe it was totally unrelated.

I tried Rocky again. She still didn't answer. I knew she wouldn't leave me hanging like this unless something was wrong. I couldn't believe I'd left her at Kiki's house with a semidead, steroid-addled lip muncher. If Mike was gnawing on my best friend, he was going to be in a world of hurt.

I ran back down the stairs, leapt the banister in a fit of adrenaline-induced athleticism, and scared the heck out of Jonah. He was trying to stuff the chicken suit into the hall closet. When I charged past him, he squawked indignantly. I wasn't slowing down. My friend might be in trouble. Vague, unexplained trouble, but trouble nonetheless.

I jumped back into the car and drove toward Rocky's house. Her battery was probably low. Or maybe her phone was charging. "She's probably at home right now, asleep already," I told myself, clutching the wheel. "That's why she hasn't called me back." I knew that was the most logical explanation. But I still couldn't stop shaking. There was something seriously wrong with Mike. He looked wrong. He smelled wrong.

He *tasted* wrong.

When I turned onto her street, I was going maybe a little faster than I should have been. I saw the bright lights of an SUV coming straight toward me from the opposite direction. They practically lased out my eyeballs. I squinted, trying to find the street despite driving blind. There was a mailbox outside my window, close enough to touch.

My wimpy little puke-scented sedan was no match for an SUV; I was about to be pulverized.

I wrenched the wheel to the right. My hyped-up reflexes overcompensated, and the car went bouncing and rattling off the road onto somebody's lawn, taking out a row of ornamental bushes before it rolled to a stop.

My hands shook so hard that I couldn't open the door, and the stench hit me again. Finally I managed to get out of the car and promptly tripped over the sorry remains of a bush half-stuck in my wheel well.

"Rocky!" I shrieked as my friend stumbled out of the SUV.

She staggered across the street with a weird shuffling gait. Fear paralyzed me; I needed to breathe but couldn't make my muscles respond. She lurched across the lawn.

She was crying. And I was pretty sure it wasn't because she'd almost run me over.

I swallowed a big gulp of air, and then I was on my feet and running toward her. At first I thought I might pass out, but when I reached her, she collapsed on me. I staggered even though she weighed practically nothing.

"Rocky! Are you okay?"

She just cried harder, so I hugged her tight. Then I started searching for bite marks. I didn't see any on her face or arms, so I ran my hands along her sides. I hoped she didn't think I was feeling her up.

"It's Bryan," she said, hiccupping. She pulled away, wiping her face with the back of her hand. "He's been shot."

I had no idea what I'd been expecting her to say, but that wasn't it.

"What—how—is he okay?" I stammered.

"I think so, but I haven't talked to him. He's in the base infirmary."

"What happened?"

"He got shot in the butt. His mom called just a couple minutes ago." Rocky blinked back tears. "I'm his girlfriend; how could he not tell me?"

Rocky was my best friend, and she deserved my support at a time like this, but all I could think to say was "He's got a bullet in his booty?"

"Yeah." She sniffled.

I started to giggle hysterically. She looked offended for about a second and then joined in.

Rocky got herself under control before I did. "His mom wants me to come over. Will you come with me?" she asked.

I wiped my streaming eyes. "Of course, Rock. Anything you want."

"You're awesome." She looked at me closely. "Hey. Your lip is bleeding."

Now that I could unload the whole sordid mess, I realized I really didn't want to talk about it. I didn't even want to think about it. I wanted to forget it had ever happened and avoid Mike for eternity. So for the first time in my life, I lied to my best friend.

I licked my lip, as if the injury was news to me. The scab had cracked open, probably during the accident. "I must have bit it when I went off the road."

Rocky looked concerned. "Can you get your car off the grass?"

"One way to find out."

I tugged the bush from my wheel and gently set the remains down on the lawn before getting into the car. It was surprisingly easy to get back on the road again, although I ran over the rest of the bushes in the process. The house remained dark; no one came outside to yell at me for decimating their shrubbery. I should probably have left a note or something, but there wasn't time.

I followed Rocky to Bryan's house. Now that I knew she was okay, I felt mostly calm. Part of me still wanted to stop and figure out what was wrong with Mike; I didn't even know where he was, and that really worried me. But Rocky needed my help. Besides, not much would change in an hour.

At least, that was what I kept telling myself.

CHAPTER seven

Bryan's mom answered the door of their tiny little ranch house. She was all puffy-faced and blotchy, like she'd been crying for the last sixty hours or so over her son's butt. This struck me as a slight overreaction.

"Oh, Roxanne," she gushed. "I'm so glad you're here."

They hugged. I hovered in the doorway, shifting from foot to foot.

"I hope it's okay that I brought Kate," Rocky said. "I thought she could be helpful."

"Of course." Mrs. Rodriguez managed to give me a smile. "Are you hungry? I've made carnitas."

My stomach growled. I couldn't remember the last time I'd had a meal that didn't come from a box or a window. "Um, sure. Thanks."

I tore into the food with the kind of table manners you develop in an eat-and-run family. But Mrs. Rodriguez started gaping at me about two bites in, so I forced myself to actually chew my food for once.

"So," I said between mouthfuls, "what's up with Bryan? Is he okay?"

"I don't know, Kate. I don't know what to think. He's . . ." Mrs. Rodriguez trailed off, shrugging.

"I'm sure he'll be okay," I said, using my most reassuring voice. "Random gunshots happen more often than you think, and usually there are no real complications."

"I'm not worried about the bullet," Mrs. Rodriguez said.

"What are you worried about, then?" I asked.

She poured herself a cup of coffee. "Bryan missed his Sunday-night check-in. He's usually good about calling, so I assumed he was out on a training mission. It was a surprise when he called me tonight from a number I didn't recognize."

"Okay," I said. "And what did he tell you?"

"He said he was under quarantine, and he couldn't talk long."

I frowned. Military docs don't quarantine shooting victims. Quarantine meant we were talking about a communicable disease, maybe even bioterrorism.

I couldn't make sense of that. "Why is he under quarantine?" I asked. "What does that have to do with a bullet wound?"

Mrs. Rodriguez took a sip. "He said he was shot during their first live-fire exercise, but the bullet just grazed him. Nothing to worry about. But when he was about to be discharged from the infirmary, they brought in some other soldiers. They were vomiting black stuff all over the place, and then they started going stiff. 'Like a dead dog, Mom,' he told me." Her hand shook and coffee sloshed out of the cup. "And then the doctors put on Hazmat suits and quarantined the whole place. He can't leave. The only reason he was even able to call was because they left the phone unattended for a minute."

"Did he touch the vomit?" I asked, managing through sheer force of will to keep my voice from shaking. "Did he tell you if he touched it?"

"I—I don't think so."

"Then he's probably safe. Unless whatever's causing it is airborne."

If it was airborne, they probably would have already issued a health alert. I would have heard about it.

I put my hand to my mouth, and it came away with a viscous red smear. The bleeding still hadn't stopped, although it was practically a trickle now. Mrs. Rodriguez handed me a napkin and I smiled at her thankfully.

"So we don't need to worry?" Rocky whispered.

I didn't know what to say. "They'll isolate Bryan from the other patients so that the chance of infection is minimal. They know what they're doing." I couldn't keep that wobble out of my voice no matter how hard I tried. "I've got to go. Now."

Rocky blinked at me. "I don't understand. . . ."

"Rock, the vomit might be infectious."

"But Bryan didn't touch it."

"Maybe not," I said, pushing my plate away. "But Jonah did."

I broke a few traffic laws on the way home, but I didn't care. It took a lot of effort to keep myself from totally breaking down or driving off the road again. I really wanted to curl up in a little ball with my blankie and let someone else deal with all this. But I couldn't.

Based on what Mrs. Rodriguez had said, I assumed we were dealing with an infectious disease. I knew more about communicable diseases than I did about football, but not by much. Part of me wanted nothing to do with my car, but I knew most infectious agents don't live for long outside the body. The infectivity ought to be gone even if the stench remained. If anyone was at risk, it was Jonah, because he'd had immediate contact with the puke.

And then there was me. If Mike had the same thing as the guys on the base and he bit me . . .

I didn't want to think about that. I needed to stay rational if I wanted to figure out what the heck was going on.

I swung into the driveway and sprinted into our house. I'd run more that night than I ever had in my life. My gym teacher would have been so proud.

Jonah wasn't in the living room. Or the kitchen. His slovenly excuse for a bedroom was empty. I slammed his door in frustration, and Dad shuffled out into the hallway, gazing at me with bleary eyes. He wore his bathrobe and Mom's old pair of pink fuzzy slippers.

"Sorry I woke you up, Dad," I said. "Nothing to worry about. Just looking for Jonah."

"What did he do this time?" Dad yawned.

I couldn't tell him. Saying it out loud would mean this was really happening.

I forced myself to sound casual. "He just took something of mine, that's all."

"Well, I'd appreciate it if you'd stop barging around like a crazy person. I have to be into the office early tomorrow."

"Sorry!" I said, pushing past him and dashing back down the stairs.

I flung open the basement door. The light was on. Thank god; I'd found him.

"Jonah?" I called.

My feeling of relief was short-lived. He didn't answer. He could be lying there unconscious and no one would know. I should have brought my med kit, but I didn't want to waste precious seconds running out to the car to get it. My brother needed me.

I ran down the stairs and turned the corner at the bottom. Then I felt something hard hit my head, and my skull flared with pain. I saw a flash of something like lightning.

Everything went dark.

CHAPTER eight

When I came to, it felt like someone had stabbed me in the frontal lobe. I pinched the bridge of my nose, as if that was going to help, and looked around. I was in my bed. Jonah sat in the yellow floral papasan chair next to me; he shoved a glass of water in my face, followed by my meds. My migraines and seizures usually came in a one-two combo.

"If you're coming to school," Jonah said, "you better get up."

"What happened?" I croaked.

I wrestled the cap off my meds with one hand and shielded my eyes ineffectually with the other. Sharp spears of light pierced my eyeballs.

"Sorry, Kate." He hung his head. "I thought you were one of my friends."

"Huh?"

"I thought you were Drew. I knew he was going to try to take me down soon. I hit you when you came downstairs, and you had a seizure. Dad was really upset."

Ahh. Jonah had been playing Assassins again. It was his favorite game ever; the point was to "kill" the other players with pretend weapons and fake poison made out of green food coloring. The last one standing won the game.

This explained the bonk, the lightning, and the look of abject shame on his face.

"What did you hit me with?"

"My sword." He pulled out a long piece of plastic pipe wrapped in powder-blue foam and secured with what looked like a roll and a half of duct tape. I'd never seen anything more ridiculous. He got that pompous, know-it-all tone he always used when talking about anything gaming related. "I'm learning swordplay, okay?"

"Jonah, that's nothing like a real sword. The weight is all wrong."

"You're an expert, huh?"

"It's just common sense, dork." I rubbed my head irritably.

"Well, it was enough to take you down."

I couldn't come up with a good response, so I didn't bother saying anything. I struggled to get up and padded over to my dresser. It only took me a minute to pop my migraine med, prepare a syringe, and inject the seizure drug. Had I missed my injection yesterday? I didn't think a bonk on the head would be enough to cause a seizure on its own.

I was feeling pretty sorry for myself until I remembered what happened to Mike. Things could be a lot worse.

"How do you feel?" I demanded. "You okay?"

"Uh ... Kate? Shouldn't I be asking you that, since you're the one who had a seizure? Dad had to carry you upstairs. He took away your car keys and your license, so don't even bother looking."

I shrugged. "I don't want to drive right now anyway. My car smells like puke."

"I'm just saying he'll want to have the seizure safety talk."

Jonah knew how much I'd wanted my license, but they won't let epileptics on the road until you can prove you're not going to lose consciousness on a regular basis. So I hadn't gotten my license until well after my seventeenth birthday, and now it looked like I was going to lose it after only two months.

Epilepsy sucks.

"Thanks for the warning," I said. "Seriously, what about you? Any vomiting? Stomach cramps? Dizziness?"

"Are you mental?"

"Let me check you out. Or I'm telling Dad you whacked me over the head with a pseudosword. I bet you edited that part out, didn't you?"

"You wouldn't."

"Try me."

He submitted to a rapid-fire physical, although he made it clear how unhappy he was about it, whining and moaning like a little girl the entire time. I ran through every exam I could think of, but I didn't find a thing wrong with him.

After Jonah went to shower, I checked myself over. Pulse, blood pressure, respiration, temperature: a full and accurate list. Everything was fine, except for my headache.

I needed to see if Mike's symptoms were progressing. I needed to be at school in case he tried to bite somebody else. And I'd promised Kiki I'd help her out later at the pancake supper she'd helped organize for homecoming. I couldn't stay home. So I dragged myself out of bed and went downstairs. Dad was sitting in the breakfast nook digging into a bowl of high-fiber cereal. He put down his magazine and waved me over.

"Hey," he said. "You gave us quite a scare. What happened?"

I decided not to tell him I might be infected with a latent virus of unknown origins and effects. "I ran all over the place, and I think it was too much for my system to handle."

Dad stirred a huge spoonful of sugar into his cereal. "And what about the medical emergency Jonah was telling me about? Something about a guy getting sick at a party?"

I shrugged. "Someone collapsed at this party at Kiki's house. I took care of him until the EMTs came."

"Is he okay?"

I wasn't sure how to answer that. Mike was probably infected with the mystery disease, which was bad. And diseased or not, he *was* the king of the Neanderthals.

"He's as good as can be expected," I finally said.

"Good." My dad smiled at me. "He's lucky you were there." Then he picked up his magazine again. "I took your car keys, by the way. And your license."

"I figured." I couldn't keep the sigh out of my voice.

"I'm sorry, Kate, but it's for your own safety. You've got an appointment with Dr. Kallas next week. We may need to adjust the meds again. And if you want the surgery . . . it's your choice."

There was a surgery that almost guaranteed to get rid of seizures like mine, but they had to open up your head and torch some neurons. Being seizure-free would have almost been worth having some surgeon grope my cerebrum. The operative word being *almost*.

"Yeah, I know." I rested my head in my hands and tried ineffectively not to look glum.

We sat for a few minutes in silence. I debated getting a slice of raisin bread, but it looked like it was all gone except for the heel. Things just weren't going my way. So I moped until Dad spoke up from behind *Physics Quarterly*. "Kate, I'm really proud of you. That guy could have died."

"Thanks, Dad." I stood up, kissed his forehead, and poured myself a cup of coffee. I didn't bother to tell him that I thought the guy actually had.

"I can't do this, Kate," Kiki said later that morning in bio.

I was still dragging despite three cups of coffee, but Kiki looked even worse. Her face was a nasty shade of green that clashed with her sweater. That worried me; I hoped she didn't have the mystery disease. I twisted in my seat to look at Mike for comparative purposes. He hadn't stopped kicking the back of my desk since he'd sat down behind me, but I'd successfully ignored him so far.

I expected one of his usual pervy comments, but he just stared until I turned away. On the good side, I was pretty sure Kiki didn't have whatever he had. His skin wasn't green; it was gray. On the bad side, I expected him to start gnawing on my braid any second now. He had that freaky intense stare thing going again. And if he didn't stop kicking my chair, I wasn't responsible for what happened.

"It's just a pig, Kiki." I pinched the bridge of my nose. It did nothing to alleviate the throbbing of my temples, but it was a nice thought anyway. "I'll do the actual cutting. Just hand me the instruments."

"You don't understand. I just can't cut up a pig!"

"Look. I'm not asking you to cut him up. I'm asking you to hand me the instruments while I cut him up. Our grades depend on this."

"The *smell*—" she started to wail, but Mrs. Mihalovic clapped for attention and cut her off.

"Okay, class. We'll be starting on the head today. Can anyone describe to me the structures you'll encounter as you penetrate the skullcap? Anyone?" She looked around, but no one was desperate enough for brownie points to volunteer. "Mr. Luzier?"

Mike stared at her vacantly. I wondered if he had bitten anyone else yet. No one in class was sporting an attractive bite mark, so I assumed not.

"Any day now, Mr. Luzier," Mrs. Mihalovic said.

"Braaaaains," Mike said. The word came out long and exaggerated, and some people laughed. Not me, of course.

She pursed her lips disapprovingly. "Very funny, Mr. Luzier. Miss Carlyle? Would you please improve upon Mr. Luzier's answer?"

Kiki made a sound like "Urk!" and ran from the lab with both hands clasped over her mouth. Mrs. Mihalovic and I exchanged long-suffering looks; I shrugged helplessly.

"I give up," she grumbled. "Just get started."

I thought about checking on Kiki, but I had no desire to hold her hair while she puked. So I went to my lab bench, strapped on my protective gear, and got to work. The whole dissection process was fascinating, and I was so into it that Kiki surprised me when she sat back down.

She leaned in confidentially. Her breath smelled like mint. "So, about last night? Thanks again for helping with . . . you know. Things could have gotten really bad if you hadn't been there."

I looked across the lab at Aaron and Mike's table. Aaron hunched over their pig while Mike stared at Mindi Skibinski's butt like he wanted to take a big bite out of it. I'd have been freaked out except it was what he usually did during lab.

"No problem." I figured it was safe to continue dissecting; Kiki wasn't really paying attention anyway. I opened the tissue surrounding the cranium with a swift stroke of my scalpel. "Pins, please."

She handed them over, taking great pains not to look. "So you remember those EMTs from the party? One of them asked me out."

"Wow. And your parents are okay with you going out with an older guy?"

"Oh, he's not my type. He's *ancient*." She grinned. "But it was still pretty flattering." Then she lowered her voice to a whisper. "He told me something interesting, though."

"What? And can you pass me the bone saw, please?"

"He said their Breathalyzer was broken. It's a good thing too, because otherwise Mike would have been in big trouble. He got cited for underage drinking once before."

"Broken?" I asked. "That's lucky."

"I know; isn't it? They said it was like he wasn't breathing at all. They tried to retest him, but he refused. Smart guy."

I removed the top of the skull, but all I could think about was Breathalyzers. They operate on airflow. Maybe Mike could hold his breath for a ridiculous amount of time, or maybe the Breathalyzer really was broken. Or maybe he hadn't been breathing. I knew that wasn't possible, but after everything I'd seen, I could almost believe it.

I didn't like this one bit. My list of possible symptoms now included black vomit, rigor mortis, semicannibalistic tendencies, and severely depressed respiration. I couldn't think of a single freaking disease that had this kind of presentation. I would have been panicking, but the military hadn't issued a health alert. Yet.

Mrs. Mihalovic walked past, shaking a finger in our direction. "Less talking, ladies. More work."

Kiki looked at me. "Strange, huh?"

"Yeah." I located the corpus callosum and sliced decisively through it. "Very."

CHAPTER
nine

The lunch line inched along at a funereal pace. I didn't really have the patience to deal with it, but I needed caffeine and sugar if I was going to remain conscious. When I got to the front, the lunch lady glared at me. She took poor nutrition as a personal affront, and my tray contained a cookie and three cans of soda.

She frowned and pointed at the Coke. "That stuff will rot your liver."

On any other day, I would have corrected her, but today I was in a hurry. I paid for the cookie and a cup of ice since the cans were still warm from their hibernation at the bottom of my locker. I'd been lobbying for pop machines in the cafeteria but hadn't won yet.

I took my change and made my way toward our usual table by the windows, but Rocky intercepted me before I sat down.

"Kate! I didn't expect to see you at lunch today. Don't you have Quiz Bowl?"

"Oh, no!" I smacked my forehead. "You're right."

My stomach sank. I couldn't believe I'd forgotten; I'd been on the team for three years. I was the president, for god's sake. I dashed for the basement, because that was how our school rolled: the perennially losing football team got an athletic wing, and the state-champion Quiz Bowl team got a four-square-foot closet in freaking Siberia.

Swannie, our faculty advisor, looked up when I hurried through the door. Her name was Ms. Swan, but she wouldn't answer to it. I thought she looked like the love child of a mad scientist and a leprechaun, with her short stature and crazy red Afro. But she was the most brilliant scientist I'd ever met, and she let me help in her lab after school sometimes. She had some big government research grants, which was unheard of for a high school chemistry teacher and pretty much elevated her to sainthood in my eyes.

"Sorry I'm late," I said. "I couldn't function any longer without a caffeine run."

She grinned and tilted her coffee cup in my direction.

"I'll let it slide this time," she said. "But don't do it again or else."

I grinned. We both knew the threat was a big joke. But I stopped smiling when I realized the rest of the team was already paired up and going over their question packets. Everyone except Mike Luzier.

I had no idea why he'd joined Quiz Bowl in the first place, but I had the sneaking suspicion that it had something to do with panting after Mindi Skibinski, who sat one table over. They spent most of our practice sessions making googly eyes at each other. As if he wasn't annoying enough already.

"We drew partners already. You're with Mike," Swannie told me. "We're reviewing the questions from State last year."

"Uh . . . okay."

The last thing I wanted was to sit down next to the lip chomper, but I couldn't come up with a good excuse not to.

He didn't move when I took the unopened question packet off the table next to him and opened it. He was too busy staring at the ceiling fan. It was his typical rude behavior and strangely reassuring.

"All right," I said. "Here's your first question: 'This disease can be transmitted from cattle to human or from human to human. Common symptoms include memory loss, gait problems, and tremors. It's one of the few infectious diseases not caused by a virus or bacteria. What is the name of the disease caused by the prion protein?'"

The answer was obvious: mad cow disease, otherwise known as Creutzfeldt-Jakob, but Mike didn't bite. No pun intended.

"Mike?" I prompted.

Still no response. The fan was much more interesting than I was, or maybe he was sleeping with his eyes open. I'd have said he was dead, but I wasn't going to make that mistake again. He was just being a tool, and it was ticking me off.

I stood up. "Swannie? Can I go get a drink?"

"You have three cans of Coke on your desk," she said. "If that's not enough, you have a serious problem."

"I dropped them on the floor," I lied. "Can't open them now."

"Ah." She shrugged. "Make it quick. We trade packets in ten."

"Okay."

I went up the stairs and down the hallway into the music wing, because they didn't have water fountains in Siberia. I didn't usually drink water because it interfered with my caffeine habit, but I decided I'd make an exception today. I wasn't lying about being thirsty. Besides, I figured the more time I spent avoiding Mike, the better.

As I was bending over to get a drink at the fountain, someone grabbed my braid and yanked. Hard. But I was used to this kind of thing. I was the class brain, after all, and I knew from experience that the worst thing to do was overreact. So I turned around slowly and said, "Is that the best you can do?"

Mike loomed over me. He held his hands over my head in what was probably meant to be a menacing fashion and said, "Gaaaaaaah!" It wasn't scary; it was ridiculous. I started giggling and couldn't stop.

Then he grabbed me. Suddenly, not laughing became a lot easier. He started dragging me across the floor toward a darkened classroom, until I realized I ought to be resisting. My shoes squeaked on the linoleum. At least his breath wasn't as bad as last time. He probably hadn't puked on any cars lately.

I fully planned on screaming once my voice decided to cooperate. Not like anyone would have heard me anyway; the music wing was deserted at this time of day. I clawed at his hands, trying to pull his fingers open so I could make a run for it.

His middle finger broke off in my palm like a dry twig.

My voice abruptly started working again. I shrieked at the top of my lungs and dropped the finger on the floor. It made a little *piff*ing sound and bounced onto my shoe; I jumped up and down like it was attacking me. Finally, my wild flailing sent it skittling across the linoleum, and it rolled to a stop next to a row of dusty lockers.

I looked up at Mike, fully expecting to see a lot of gushing blood and yuck, but there was nothing. Just a cloud of dust particles hanging in the air over his four-fingered hand and a look of complete confusion on his face.

It didn't last long. He bared his teeth, revealing blue gums. I was still gaping when he grabbed me again.

"Hey!" yelled a deep voice from down the hall.

I turned, half expecting to see Aaron. But it wasn't him. It was my brother.

"Leave my sister alone!" He stalked down the hallway toward us, clenching his scrawny fists.

Mike froze, his nine fingers digging into my shoulders. He looked as surprised as I felt. Jonah was the kind of guy who strained to open a jar of pickles. He wasn't someone you expected random heroics from.

"Huh?" Mike said, his forehead wrinkling.

"Leave her alone!" Jonah was red-faced with anger. "Or I'll beat the crap out of you!"

Mike laughed, low and rumbly. He released my shoulders, which was nice, and took a step toward Jonah, which wasn't. I couldn't let my brother get clobbered. He had no idea what he was dealing with. I didn't either, but standing there in the hallway with a severed finger at my feet, I couldn't help but think that the virus was creating . . . zombies. There. I'd thought it. And going into zombie territory was stupid.

I stepped between them. Mike's eyes snapped to my face, and I barely managed not to shrink away from him. But he didn't try to drag me off again. He smelled me instead. His nostrils flared as he sniffed the air between us and licked his lips.

At that point I was more than willing to turn tail and run, but not Jonah. He might have been half Mike's size, but he was ready for a fight.

I grabbed him by the arm. "We're leaving."

"I'm not letting him get away with this," Jonah said. "I'm sick of bullies like him."

I couldn't tell him about the finger. If I said it out loud, that would make it real. I'd fall apart, right here in the hallway, and Mike would probably eat me midhysteria. I had to do something to stop Jonah, though.

"What's that? Over there?" I pointed vaguely. And it worked. Mike turned slowly around to look.

"Jonah," I whispered, tearing up. I wasn't the crying type, but right now I wasn't sure whether I was more afraid *of* Mike or afraid *for* him. "Let's go."

Jonah clenched his jaw and nodded. I didn't resist when he took my arm and led me away, but I couldn't keep from glancing over my shoulder. Mike hadn't even noticed us leave. He was too busy looking around on the floor. I saw his finger, half underneath a locker in a sea of dust bunnies, but I decided not to point it out to him.

Once we turned the corner into the main hallway, I felt a little better. I pulled away from Jonah, because let's face it, neither of us needed to be seen skipping through the halls arm in arm with our sibling.

"You okay?" he asked.

"Yeah, thanks." Now that we were safe, I sounded remarkably calm. I began to think I should take up acting.

"I sure showed him." He nodded. "He won't be bothering you anymore."

As his older sister, I should have laughed at that. But he had just saved me from being groped by the nine-fingered wonder, so

I didn't. Instead, I said, "Yeah. Um . . . I should get back to Quiz Bowl."

"I'll walk you back."

"What are you doing here?" I asked as we headed for the stairs.

He shrugged. "Some guys kinda duct-taped me to the toilet. I just got loose."

I sighed. "Oh, Jonah. Are you okay?"

He nodded. "Fine. They didn't tape any skin, which I thought was nice. Of course, I'm still hacking into their computers tonight."

I held out my palm. He smacked it.

Jonah dropped me off and headed for the cafeteria before they stopped serving lunch. I looked through the window into the Quiz Bowl practice room. Thankfully, Mike's seat was empty. For the moment, I was safe.

I leaned against the door to the supply closet across the hall until I stopped shaking. It took a long time, probably because I couldn't stop scanning the hallway for Mike.

Finally, I squared my shoulders and stood up. Time to go back to Quiz Bowl, even though my mind wasn't on those questions. I clearly needed to get to the bottom of this mystery illness— preferably before anyone else lost any more fingers.

CHAPTER
ten

I had a late lunch period, so I only needed to endure AP History and Calculus II before I was free to put my plan into action. The wait was still torturous; I practically sprinted for my locker after the final bell.

Aaron was leaning against it. For a minute, I thought I must have gone down the wrong hallway again, because I wasn't so good with directions. But then I realized he was probably there on purpose and I had to keep from squealing. He was wearing my favorite T-shirt, the green one, and a lock of hair hung in his eyes. It was ridiculously endearing. As I got closer, I noticed his backpack tossed carelessly at his feet. I could see the cover of a familiar book inside—the same anatomy and physiology text I'd been reading.

I was in love.

"Hey, Kate. Have you seen Mike?" he asked, a worried furrow between his brows.

I knew I should tell Aaron about the finger, but what if he didn't believe me? I couldn't believe it, and I'd seen it myself. He'd probably think I was on drugs. Wouldn't blame him, either.

I cleared my throat. "Not . . . uh . . . not for a while."

"Damn." He ran a hand through his hair. "This is bad. Really bad."

"Really?"

My voice came out all squeaky, but he didn't seem to notice. He pushed off the locker and leaned close, his face inches from mine. I swallowed audibly, overcome by a heady mixture of adoration, lust, and complete and utter terror. Would he kiss me? Did I want him to?

He looked deep into my eyes and said, "All of them."

I blinked. "Huh?"

"Coach injected the defensive linemen. Even the third-string guys who almost never make the field. He told them it was B twelve."

"Aaron," I said, barely resisting the urge to brush the hair out of his eyes, "I don't know whether this whole thing is linked to the injections or not. I found out about some other cases with the same symptoms, so it sounds like we're looking at an infectious disease. I don't know if it's spreading via those vials, or—"

"Logan Smith puked up the black stuff last night. Just like

Mike. And he got the shot too." He let his head fall back against my locker. The bang made me jump. "What are we going to do?"

"Are you sure? Are you positive?"

"I had to drag it out of him, but yeah. Logan told me. If you saw him for yourself, you wouldn't doubt it for a minute. He doesn't look good. I think he went home after third period."

"Is anyone else sick?"

I didn't have many classes with the other football players, so the only time I really saw them was at practice. I passed them in the halls, of course, but my schedule was so packed that I barely had time to pee, let alone conduct surreptitious surveillance.

"Wisniewski, Clements, Wade, LaBianca, and Johnson all stayed home today. I've spoken with a few other guys, none of whom were injected with anything. Coach just gave them some lame advice and sent them packing like he did with me."

He held out his hand, and I took it. There was a moment of heart-stopping panic during which I wondered if I had misread yet another social situation, before his fingers folded over mine. He probably just needed some friendly reassurance. Or maybe I'd been magically transported into a musical, and we were about to break into a song-and-dance number. I'd believe that before I'd believe he was interested in me.

I cleared my throat and lifted my eyes from our intertwined fingers. They looked good together. "Um . . . I could help. If you want."

"Thanks, Kate. You're the best."

I shuffled uncomfortably. I didn't know how to interpret this. Instead of AP Latin, I should have taken Talking to Boys Without Stammering.

"All right," I said, getting back to business. "We need to get our hands on one of those vials. I think they might really be steroids, but maybe they're tainted with a virus or something. If I figure out what it is, we could notify the health department. Dr. Ho could probably get us in touch with the right people."

"Why wait? Let's talk to him now."

I snorted. "You really think he's going to listen when we start spouting off conspiracy theories about some drug that makes people's fingers fall off? I need proof."

"I'm sorry?" he said. "You lost me at the finger part. Aren't we talking like hepatitis or something? That seems like the most logical explanation, doesn't it?"

"I don't know." I didn't want to get into the finger-related details, not now. We were getting along so well, and I wanted to enjoy it while it lasted. "We need those vials if we're going to find out for sure."

"Well," he said slowly, "I am the team captain."

"Do you have a key?"

He didn't answer, just released my hand, reached into his backpack, and produced a key ring. It wasn't the size of a steering wheel, which was a nice change.

"Let's steal some drugs," he said.

* * *

Coach's office had never been the neatest place in the world. Today it had been ransacked. The filing cabinets stood open, papers dumped all over the floor. The shelving unit hung cockeyed from one bracket, trophies shattered underneath. There was a vaguely head-shaped indentation in the wall behind the desk.

"What do you think happened?" I asked in a hushed voice, closing the door behind us.

"Dunno." Aaron nudged a pile of papers out of the way with his foot. "Nothing good."

I made my way past the overturned Gatorade cart and the sticky floor underneath. The medical cabinet was badly dented. It looked like someone had taken a sledgehammer to it. Too bad the lock was intact.

"I think we should be able to pry that open if we find something strong enough," I said, pointing at a bent corner.

Aaron nodded. "I'm on it."

I went through the desk while Aaron took the floor. Coach had three Little Mermaid DVDs in the middle drawer. I tried to shake the mental images of his secret life as a closet mermaid lover, but they were tough to get out of my head.

I paused midsearch. Inspiration struck; I felt the rush that always came with solving a problem or acing a test. It felt kind of like I imagined a runner's high must feel, except in my case it was a thinker's high. I grabbed the first-aid kit and rummaged through a small mountain of gauze and eight rolls of unopened medical tape. And there they were.

"Scissors?" Aaron asked when I held them up. "What're you going to do, cut the door open?"

"They're heavy-duty bandage scissors. They're about as sturdy as a crowbar. If you can break them, I'll eat my shoe."

"You're brilliant," he said, and when the door popped open, I had to agree.

The tray of vials was still on the shelf. A lot of the slots were empty now, which horrified me. I stooped to pick it up, but my hands shook from the heady combination of mystery illness plus breaking and entering multiplied by close proximity to Aaron. Thinking about this made me shake so hard that one of the vials leapt out of the tray and rolled under the desk.

"Aw, man." I smacked my forehead.

We reached for it at the same time, and our heads collided. Now my skull hurt like blazes, but at least it took my mind off my lip—the scab was ginormous, which reduced my attractiveness level from minuscule to nonexistent.

"I'm sorry. Are you okay? I didn't mean to do that," I babbled. I hated babblers, and I was turning into one. Then Aaron put his hand on my arm, which only intensified my need to spew nonsense. "I'm such a klutz. My brother hit me on the head with a fake sword the other night and actually knocked me unconscious, which you'd think wouldn't be possible given the tensile strength of plastic pipe, only with my luck it's all too possible. I mean, between that and when I ran my car off the road and totally smashed this guy's bushes into—"

He kissed me.

I couldn't concentrate enough to worry. His mouth was warm, and he tasted like mint, and he did this thing with his tongue that was absolutely divine. His arms slid around my shoulders and held me, tight but not too tight. I made one little sound of submission and that was it. All rational thought went out the window.

I didn't know how long we kissed. It was even better than I'd imagined.

I heard a sound from the hallway, but I was busy. I'd get back to my usual hypervigilance later. But then I became aware of a familiar, fetid scent. It smelled like toasted poop, but with a new undertone of corruption, like the poop had been left to rot in the sun for a couple of days and got all slimy and putrid.

The doorknob rattled and we froze, staring into each other's eyes. Aaron held a finger to his mouth. As if I needed the instructions. If we got caught in here, we'd be in trouble. I was having a hard enough time dealing with the shame of my demerit; detention might kill me outright.

Besides, I knew what that smell meant, and I had no desire to see any more regurgitory displays.

The smell finally got to Aaron. He started to retch; he hadn't been exposed to the stink before and wasn't used to it like I was. I clapped a hand over his mouth in an attempt to muffle the sound. I knew he might puke on me, but I decided I'd rather deal with that than risk getting mauled by my ex-fling.

The knob stopped rattling. There was a halfhearted knock at

the door, and then nothing else. I heard the sound of feet shuffling slowly away down the hall. The smell didn't diminish, but breathing through my mouth made it almost bearable.

I removed my hand from Aaron's mouth. I really wanted to wipe his germs off, but I remembered how loud the towel dispenser was and didn't want to risk it until I was sure we were in the clear.

We stood there a long time, or at least it felt long. My hand started to dry. I pulled two paper towels from the dispenser. The screech was loud enough to wake Tutankhamen, but no one came to investigate. I handed Aaron a towel to clean his face and used the other one to wipe my hand.

"I'm sorry," he said. "What's that smell? It's horrible."

"I think someone puked out in the hall. Like, um . . . maybe Mike. When he threw up on my car, it pretty much smelled the same. I told you about that, didn't I?"

"Yeah, you did. I should go out to help him," he said. I waited, but he didn't move. I realized he was really freaked out, which made me feel better for some reason. "I have to admit—I thought you were exaggerating. I know you're wicked smart; it just sounded a little over-the-top."

"Well, I wasn't. Exaggerating, I mean."

Then he said, "Hey, I think you're bleeding."

My hand flew up to my mouth. He was right, and Coach wasn't a Kleenex-on-the-desk kind of guy. I kept checking my pockets, as if persistence might make a tissue miraculously materialize in one of them. Aaron gave me another paper towel instead. And then I felt stupid.

I pressed it to my mouth and mumbled, "Thanks."

"What happened?" he asked. "To your mouth, I mean."

"Mike bit me at Kiki's party. And I'm really not exaggerating this time."

"Bit you?" His voice dropped into a growl. "I think Mike and I are going to have a little talk."

"Why?" I squeaked. "I really didn't intend to kiss him. Again, I mean. I know it's kind of weird, since I had that fling with him a couple of months ago, and now there's . . . you and . . . us. Oh god. I don't know what I mean, and now I'm babbling. I just don't want you to think I'm—"

"I think you're cool," he said firmly. "And I know how Mike gets when he drinks." I blushed. "I've got to go find him."

I'd just taken a deep breath, preparing to say the Z-word, when what he'd said finally registered.

"Uh . . . why?"

"He needs to apologize to you. I don't know what his problem is, but some things you just don't do. Know what I mean?"

Aaron flung the door open before I could answer. It was probably for the best. If he'd had a hard time believing me when I told him about the puke, I wasn't sure how to convince him that this virus made people's fingers fall off and turned them into cannibals.

He stepped over the puddle of puke, holding his hand over his mouth and nose. "I'll text you later, okay? You can take care of the vials from here, right?"

"Yeah. Sure. Later."

My verbal skills were astounding.

The door closed behind him. I was in a complete emotional tizzy, or I would have been if I'd had the time. But now I had even more motivation to take action. I had to identify the disease vector I might have accidentally transmitted to the only decent guy who would ever like me despite the fact that I had snarly hair, bad glasses, and the social aptitude of the average chimpanzee. If this virus was transmitted by bodily fluid, I had probably contracted it when Mike bit me.

I snatched three vials, pulled a Ziploc bag out of my backpack, and sealed them carefully inside. I might not have been great with the romance thing, but no one was going to outscience me. Especially when there was a hot boy at stake.

CHAPTER eleven

I took the vials straight to the chem lab. I had about an hour before I was supposed to volunteer at the pancake supper, and I was feeling the pressure. That was the worst thing about being friends with Kiki: she inflicted her do-goodery on people. No way would I have volunteered for this stupid thing if she hadn't begged. A lot of the football team would be there since it was an official homecoming week event, though, so it was good for me to be there too.

I turned the corner to the science wing, and Swannie came out of the lab with a cardboard box precariously balanced on one shoulder. It was so big she could have fit inside with room to spare. She'd just finished a project on muscular responses in mice and was probably packing it up to make way for something new. I couldn't wait to hear what we were doing next, but I didn't have time to listen to a whole research plan.

"Let me help you with that," I offered.

She snatched the box away before I could touch it.

"I've got it," she said. "You working on something fun?"

"Um . . . that's not exactly the word I'd use." I sighed. "You don't mind, do you?"

"Of course not. My lab is your lab. I owe you for sectioning all those mice. I wouldn't have been able to finish that project without you, you know."

I beamed. "It was my pleasure. Seriously."

She shifted the box. "I've got to go before my shoulder falls off. But you'll have to tell me what you're working on later. Maybe I can give you some advice. Not like you need any, but it makes me feel important."

"Thanks," I said. "I'll definitely take you up on it."

She left the door open for me. It was too bad; I got a little thrill every time I used my key. Swannie had made me one when I was helping her with the mice. Being a suck-up really did have its advantages.

Technically, the room was supposed to be a storage area, but Swannie had converted it to her own personal lab. It was crammed with centrifuges and pipettes, and it was all Swannie's. She'd paid for it using her government funding. If I hadn't wanted to be a doctor so badly, I'd have wanted to be her when I grew up.

Unfortunately, I wasn't sure what to do now that I was here. I stared down at the vials. After a minute or so, I realized that the most important thing was to isolate the virus or bacteria. It didn't really matter if Coach thought he was shooting the players up with a steroid, B12, or lighter fluid. The most pressing danger to my players was the virus. All I needed to do was prove it existed, and then I could go to the authorities.

That meant it was time for some cell cultures.

About an hour later, I finished setting up the incubators and took off my gloves. I was surprised to actually be done on time; I always got lost in my work way too easily. I used to set an alarm when I worked on mice for Swannie, because otherwise I'd sit down at the bench for a couple of minutes, and then I'd look up and it would be four in the morning already. I was lucky my parents understood my workaholic tendencies.

The cultures needed to sit overnight. I'd check them in the morning. If they grew, I'd picture-mail the evidence over to the Ho and ask him for advice. He'd know what to do.

Now... time for pancakes.

Kiki and I were supposed to meet in the cafeteria. I opened the doors right on time, feeling pretty proud of myself. But then I started wondering if maybe I'd made a mistake. The cafeteria lights were off; the only illumination came from the red glow of the exit sign. The portable griddle sat in pieces at the end of the room. The caf was a sea of empty putty-colored tables, conspicuously devoid of volunteers.

Then Kiki walked through the door from the kitchen, and I breathed a sigh of relief. As soon as she saw me, she dropped an entire armful of paper products on the floor and waded through them to hug me.

"Oh, Kate, I'm so glad you're here!" she wailed, brushing hair out of her red, sweaty face—and somehow still managing to look good. "The squad was supposed to be here at three-thirty, and none of them showed. I tried to call, but no one's answering. They all better have darn good reasons for standing me up, or I'll bench them. I'm so . . . so . . . pissed!"

"It's okay." I put a hand on her shoulder. "It's just pancakes, Kiki. We can handle pancakes."

"But this is the big cheer-sponsored homecoming event. How does it look if none of the cheerleaders show up?"

"I don't think anyone will mind so long as there's food to eat. Just point me toward the cook tables and everything will be fine."

The griddle went together easily, because I was one of those people who actually followed instruction manuals. Within ten minutes, I was ready to switch it on. I'd never made pancakes before, but I was better than I'd expected after a few practice runs. It was like following a lab protocol, a process requiring impeccable timing and precise measurements. I devised a system to keep the line moving steadily while maintaining food temperature at acceptable levels. When Kiki brought me the batter, I tried to explain it to her, but her eyes glazed over about three words in. People just didn't appreciate my talent.

A couple of the cheerleaders finally showed up just in time to serve as cashiers, with some lame excuse about car trouble. Kiki read them the riot act; I probably would have grumped at them too if I hadn't been having fun despite myself. We opened at five o'clock and were immediately swamped. I fired off pancakes as quickly as I did Quiz Bowl answers, but the line kept growing anyway. People couldn't wait to fork over eight bucks for my cooking. I could probably have funded my college education with my mad pancake skills, but this money would be used to buy the cheerleaders new go-go boots. We all had our priorities.

I was so busy that the only time I saw my players was when I was filling their plates. None of them seemed sick, nor did anyone loom over me like Count Chocula on crack. I saw a lot of chalky gray skin tones, but it was mid-October in the Midwest, so I wasn't sure whether to blame their complexions on the mystery disease or our sucky weather. Mike didn't show.

I flipped pancakes at precisely timed intervals, and the line marched on. I took two paces to the left, squirted out six puddles of batter in row one, flipped row three, served row five, squirted out six more puddles, and so on. I had pancake making down to an art form.

Then I heard an improper sizzle.

My technique was so refined that I knew something was wrong. It was too early for row two to be sizzling, too late for row four. I didn't have any sausages cooking right now.

I did, however, have a hand on my griddle.

It belonged to a woman with a mom bob, a vacant stare, and an athletic booster pin. She leaned across the griddle to offer me her plate, bracing herself with one hand. Palm down. Next to a bubbling pancake. I figured she must be an amputee, but I didn't smell burning plastic. It smelled kinda like bacon, actually.

I looked around to see if anyone else had noticed, but people were remarkably unobservant. A couple of guys from the offensive line stood behind her; they were busy discussing farts in great detail. Talk about offensive.

"Kate, you better take those sausages off the grill," Kiki said from the toast and juice station. "I think they're burning."

I didn't want to tell her it was the scent of fried hand. And I really didn't want to embarrass this woman by drawing attention to her disability, so I leaned closer and said, "Ma'am? Could you please move your hand?"

When she opened her mouth, a trickle of black gunk spilled out. There wasn't a lot, so the stench wasn't totally overwhelming, but I could smell it if I concentrated. Not like I was trying to smell it, because I wasn't that masochistic.

She said, "Uuuuuh."

Oh bleep. It was spreading.

This woman might have been grilling her hand on my griddle, but the reality hadn't quite hit me yet. I calmly scraped her skin off the hot metal with my spatula. Good thing I was so meticulous with the cooking spray; it came off without leaving much flesh behind.

Still. Ewww.

She kept staring at me. I held my spatula in what I imagined was a defensive posture, but she just held out her empty plate. The gesture was strangely reassuring. No way she could be a zombie, not if she wanted pancakes. Row four was torched by now, so I gave her some from row two. She shambled off peacefully.

My heart started hammering. It was one thing to know that a bunch of far-off military guys had the mystery disease, but watching it spread right in front of you was something completely different. I knew I was only hours away from some lab results, but in the meantime? I was a cardiovascular incident waiting to happen.

I was so busy obsessing about the possibility of a heart attack that I completely disregarded the possibility of a seizure. My epileptic episodes weren't usually linked to my blood pressure, but there's a first time for everything. I felt pretty sheepish when I came to a couple of minutes later with my head crooked uncomfortably against the wall and my feet sprawled halfway to the juice station.

"Oh my god, Kate, can you hear me?" Kiki crouched over me, her hair tickling my nose.

I sneezed. "I'm okay." I flailed around in an uncoordinated attempt to stand up. I had to get the rest of the pancakes off the griddle before someone got a nice helping of hand flambé. "It's just a seizure. I used to have them all the time, remember?"

"Yeah, but they're still freaky." She took my arm and helped me up. I looked around, trying to get my bearings. Everyone in the room stared at me like they expected me to grow fangs and sparkle.

"I'm okay." I shook Kiki's arm free.

"Please sit down, Kate. You're overdue for a break, and the line's slowing anyway."

"But . . ." There were still about ten people in line. I couldn't let them eat anything cooked on that griddle. But there was no way for me to explain why without sounding like a total wack job.

I could only think of one way to stop the grill from being used again. I flung my arm out, knocking over the last jug of batter in the building.

It fell in a slow-motion arc, or at least that was what it felt like. "Nooooo!" Kiki yelled, and leapt for it with her arms outstretched. But she was too late. The jug hit the floor with a tremendous *sploosh*. Within seconds, we stood in a sea of batter dotted with a bunch of dust-bunny floaters.

Kiki shot me a stricken glance. So I weaved a little on my feet to illustrate how shaky the seizure had left me. Her expression instantly changed from exasperation to concern, and I couldn't help but feel guilty for manipulating her like this, even if it was for the greater good.

"Come sit down," she said, taking my arm. "Don't worry about the pancakes. If anybody wants seconds, they can eat toast and sausages. Let me get you some juice."

She parked me in a corner with a glass of oj. It did nothing to get the image of the frying hand out of my head, but at least now I wasn't dehydrated and freaked out. I was just freaked out. It was a minor improvement, but I'd take what I could get.

"Okay," Kiki said, patting my leg. "You stay here while the girls take down the griddle."

"I can help."

I started to stand, but she pushed me back into my seat.

"Absolutely not. They need to pull a little extra weight since they were so late. You can supervise if you want." She grinned at me before walking off.

I wasn't so good at following orders. Besides, lounging in an uncomfortable cafeteria chair wasn't going to make my post-seizure headache go away. The best thing to do was to distract myself until the pounding subsided. So I helped Mindi and Lacey scrape down the griddle and dismantle it. I felt much better as I took the tray of cooking utensils into the kitchen to be washed. No one would accidentally ingest human flesh on my watch.

I turned on the water, and someone grabbed my shoulder from behind. I whipped around with a wet spatula in one hand, spraying water all over the place. I didn't really think soapy water would discourage an attacker, but it was all I could come up with on short notice.

"Hey!" Kiki yelled right in my face.

"Sorry! You scared me," I said.

"No problem." She frowned. "I thought I told you to sit down. Do I have to yell at you for not following my orders?"

"I'm really okay, Kiki. If you'd drop the whole epilepsy subject, I'd really appreciate it. It's kind of embarrassing."

"Deal." She picked up a towel and started wiping the water off the floor. "Hey, maybe you can help me."

"Help with what?" I asked.

"I need someone to lock the cash boxes in the principal's office. I'd do it myself, but . . ." She blushed. "Logan offered to take me home, and he's got to leave now. Do you mind?"

"Logan?" I turned.

Logan Smith stood by the registers with his hands in his pockets. From a distance, he looked pretty good, considering that he'd recently been puking up black mucus. In fact, he looked so normal that I started to wonder if Aaron had been wrong. It put me in an awkward situation, because I wasn't sure if I should let Kiki ride home alone with him. It might be dangerous.

Then I stopped myself. Logan was a genuinely nice guy, and Mike wasn't. That had nothing to do with the virus. So why shouldn't Kiki go out with him? I could see why she liked him; they were both really popular but didn't have a stick up their butts about it. They'd make a great couple.

It was a good thing I was a quick thinker, because I ran through this entire deductive process in a matter of seconds. "Yeah, I can take care of it," I said. "No problem."

"Are you sure you feel okay? Because I can tell him I've got to stay."

"I'm absolutely sure! Go and have a good time."

She kissed my cheek. "You are such a doll. You deserve to be an honorary cheerleader for this."

I suppressed my urge to snort. "Go before Logan turns into a pumpkin or something. Later, Logan!"

I waved to him, and he held up his hand. The gesture was reassuring in its normalcy. No zombie would ever wave like that.

And I didn't believe in zombies anyway.

Once I dragged all the cash boxes to the principal's office and locked them inside, I realized I had no way home. It was hard going back to a carless state after having one for a while.

All the cheerleaders had left. I could walk—if I took the shortcut through the woods behind the school, it only took about ten minutes. But it was dark now.

Besides, now that I had accidentally introduced the Z-word to my mental vocab, I couldn't get it out. And I knew what happened to pretty young high schoolers who went out into zombie-infested streets. I could only imagine that something similar happened to socially awkward, braided high schoolers.

I texted Rocky and waited for ten minutes, tapping my foot impatiently. No response. So then I called. Her phone was off. I tried her house, but no one answered there either. I wanted to call Aaron, only I didn't know his number.

So I called home.

"Yo," my brother answered. He thought he was street.

"Hey, Jonah. Can I talk to Dad?"

"Nope."

"Come on. Don't be a jerk."

"Seriously, he's not here. He's got some meeting thing tonight. He called to say we shouldn't wait for dinner because he's going to be superlate."

"Damn."

"Damn" was an understatement. I didn't want to die young in a freak zombie attack. I mean, sure, I was glad I'd had a chance to kiss Aaron before my untimely demise, but I hoped there were more kisses where that one came from.

"What's wrong?" Now Jonah sounded alarmed. "Has that stupid jock been bothering you again?"

"No." The pressure was suddenly too much to bear. My voice came out all shaky and teary-sounding, so I had to swallow and try again. "I'm stuck at school, and I don't want to walk home by myself. I'm—I'm not feeling so good. I had a seizure. I know I'm being a total wuss, but—"

"Kate?"

"Yeah?"

"Shut up. I'm coming to get you."

And then he hung up. It was very dramatic and also very stupid, because he didn't know exactly where I was. I was tempted to let him wander around the school for a while, but then I'd have to sit and wait for him to find me. Patience wasn't my virtue. I called him back and told him where to pick me up.

Jonah was fifteen, so he only had a learner's permit; he wouldn't get his license for another couple months. Frankly, he was lucky he still had the permit after he put Dad's car into drive instead of reverse and took the whole garage off the foundation. So I was understandably freaked when he cruised up in my car. Maybe it smelled like puke and I couldn't drive it right now, but if he crashed it, I would not be happy.

He stopped in the bus loop, and I stalked out of the school. At least I was pissed enough not to be even remotely worried I might be the victim of a bite-and-run. There's a bright side to every situation.

He rolled down the window. "Hey, sis. Want a ride?"

"I can't believe you took my car!" I snapped. "What did you hit on the way here? And you'd better be careful. If the cops pull us over, you'll be in big trouble. You're supposed to have a licensed adult in the car at all times."

Jonah's face fell. "I didn't hit anything. And Drew has his license. We're going to drop him off on the way home."

His friend smiled at me hopefully from the backseat. His face was one big zit.

I scowled at them both. "I said 'adult.'"

"Just get in the car, Kate." He leaned over and opened the passenger door. "I came here to help keep you safe; I'm not going to wrap you around a tree."

I got in the car.

Drew lived just down the street; we dropped him off and then headed home. By the time we turned off Washington Avenue into my subdivision, it was raining so hard that I could barely see the yellow line dividing the lanes. Unfortunately, our neighborhood was one of those places where streetlights have been outlawed in the interest of ambience. We had cutesy little lanterns instead. The ambience would probably have been great, except you couldn't see a darned thing.

So I couldn't be blamed for screaming when someone appeared abruptly in the half-moon of the headlights.

"Jonah! Watch out!"

I had just enough time to see a familiar beefy face topped by a baseball cap before we ran him over.

The car bounced so violently that my teeth snapped closed on my tongue and my mouth filled with blood. Jonah slammed on the brakes, but we were going too fast. The car screeched to a stop, but not before we were tossed around by another thump as the back tires passed over the body too.

"Holy crap!" Jonah shouted.

He threw the car into park while it was still moving. We jerked to a stop, jouncing me around in my seat, and barely missed an ornamental lantern.

"I—I think that was Coach," I stammered. "I'd been wondering where he was."

And now I knew. He was decorating the pavement on my street.

"Oh god . . . I can't get my seat belt off."

Jonah didn't have years of experience stalking the Red Cross like I did. If Coach needed medical attention, I was the logical one to give it.

"Stay here," I ordered. "I'll go . . . check on him."

"No!"

"Stay here!" I opened the door before he had time to argue any further. "Keep the window open; I'll shout if I need help. I might need you to bring the car closer."

I smiled reassuringly because that was what you were supposed to do in situations like this. Then I got out of the car, shielding my glasses from the rain with one hand.

Coach wasn't in the road; the only thing left on the pavement was his shoe. With shaking hands, I picked it up.

His foot was still inside.

I was remarkably calm. At least it wasn't spurting; I began to consider the non-gush factor the most beneficial side effect of zombieness. Because standing there in the middle of the street with a severed foot in my hand, I pretty much bought into the whole zombie idea for good.

The virus? It was a zombie virus.

There just wasn't any other workable explanation.

I was halfway across the street when my cell beeped. I checked out the text just in case. If Rocky was stuck in her house with a million rabid zombies at the door, I wanted to know.

It said, *Almost forgot to ask you to h-coming. Interested? Aaron.*

I stood there and gaped for a second. Then I did the unthinkable. I shut the phone without answering. I'd squeal later, provided we were both still alive. Right now? I had to see Coach for myself. I needed some kind of evidence to prove to everyone else that the zombies were real. If I showed them the foot, they'd just think I was a grave robber.

I shielded my eyes from the rain and inched toward the shadowy ditch. The closest lantern was about twenty feet away, and it adequately illuminated an area about the size of a postage stamp. My heart thumped at breakneck speed, and my instincts screamed that this was in no way a good idea. But I had his foot. He had a total handicap when it came to chasing me down.

I heard a wet rustle in the pile of leaves clogging the bottom of the ditch, but I couldn't see very well since I was backlit. I took another half step forward and craned my neck like a little head jiggle was going to miraculously give me the ability to see in the dark.

"Coach?" I squeaked.

"Graaable." Coach's voice drew out into a rusty croak. Total stereotypical zombie speech pattern.

"What?" No answer from the ditch. "Coach, are you okay?" I spoke slowly and deliberately, like he was stupid instead of undead. Which only resulted in my feeling stupid.

When the response came, it was so quiet that I edged closer to the ditch in an attempt to hear him better. I knew it was stupid, but I couldn't help myself.

"Bite . . ."

At this point, I realized I was half stooped in front of a ditch containing a flesh-eating monster, and this was probably a bad idea. That conclusion was only made more obvious when Coach thrashed out of the leaves at me. I scrambled backward, but he grabbed my ankle before I could get away. One jerk of the foot and I toppled into a puddle and sprayed water into my face, making myself even blinder than usual.

When my vision finally cleared, I kind of felt like splashing myself in the eyes again. Coach was still attached to my ankle, and he looked totally freak show. His skin was mottled and his nose was barely attached to his face. Ink still tinted his lower lip blue. An honest-to-god tire track ran across his torso and off his right shoulder, and his left leg ended about midshin, but he didn't even seem to notice.

He probably outweighed me by about a hundred pounds, so when he tried to pull himself out of the ditch by my foot, we both started sliding down the muddy bank. I scrabbled for a handhold; my fingers raked the soft ground without accomplishing much. Coach snarled and sank his teeth into the sole of my shoe, like he just couldn't wait to devour me and needed to start while we were in the middle of a miniature mudslide. I kicked and flailed in an attempt to shake him loose and tried to climb back up at the same time. I didn't have much success on either front.

When somebody grabbed me under the armpits, I thrust my

head back as fast as I could and felt pretty triumphant when it hit something hard. Even if it did hurt like blazes.

"Damn it, Kate, that was my kneecap!" Jonah yelled. He wrapped his arms around my torso and pulled, but Coach's teeth were wedged in my shoe and the guy wasn't exactly light. We didn't budge. So Jonah pulled harder.

I could feel my vertebrae popping into place; there's nothing like zombie chiropractic to take away your back pain. I choked down hysterical laughter as Jonah towed us toward the street, grunting with effort. Coach wouldn't let go of my shoe even though he was being dragged belly-down through the mud; he was like one of those little yip-yap dogs with a chew toy.

Once we got to the pavement, Jonah said, "I'll get my sword!"

"Wait!" I shrieked. "Don't leave me with him!"

But he wasn't listening. He dropped me. My butt splatted into a big puddle of muddy water, spraying Coach right in the face. He yanked me toward him, mud streaming into his open eyes. He didn't blink. I dug my fingers into the grating of a convenient sewer drain and held on so he couldn't drag me away and eat me raw.

"That sword isn't going to do jack! Run him down with the car!" I shouted, kicking Coach right on the bridge of the nose. I heard something crack, but he didn't pause. He was too busy shoving my foot into his mouth. And if that wasn't gross enough, he began gnawing a hole in my shoe. It was old and worn; the canvas gave way all too quickly. I felt his fingers scrabbling inside as he ripped off the sole, slowly working his way inside to the meat of my foot.

I realized then that I was still holding on to *his* foot, so I threw it at him. It bounced off his head but otherwise didn't really accomplish anything except that now I wasn't holding it, and that was awfully nice.

The sole came free with a deafening rip. I shoved his chest with my other foot, but Coach wouldn't let go. I swore I heard his stomach rumble.

"Jonah!" I squinched my toes up as high as they'd go as Coach tried to worm his mouth up into the remains of my shoe, search-ing for flesh. His teeth snagged on my sock. "Hurry!"

Jonah threw the car into reverse and took off with a squeal of tires, leaving streaks of rubber so long and dark that I could see them clearly despite the cruddy lighting and the rain. I prayed he wouldn't swerve at the last minute and run me over by mistake.

He hit Coach fast enough to roll him under the car. Lucky for me, Coach released my foot when the front tires passed over his torso, but the impact still wrenched my ankle around and popped my kneecap out of place. I couldn't keep from screaming.

I scrambled to my feet and lurched for the car, dragging the shredded remains of my shoe. My leg shrieked with pain; I had to drop down to the ground and scramble through the puddles on my hands and one working leg. I got soaked through and caked with gunk, but it was better than being cannibalized. I grabbed

Coach's foot off the pavement as I lurched past, because even in a situation like this I wasn't going to waste the opportunity to retrieve a sample.

I locked myself in the car and immediately performed a zombie status check. Coach was nowhere to be seen. I looked in all the mirrors, mashing my face up against the window and repeating, "Where is he? Ohmygod, where did he go? Where is he, Jonah?"

My brother put his arms around me and wouldn't let go until I calmed down.

"Coach is a zombie, isn't he?" Jonah asked when I could breathe again.

I tried to scoff. "Not exactly. If you're looking for a scientifically accurate explanation, I think he has a virus that—"

"Bull! He's a freaking zombie, Kate. I've played enough *Resident Evil* to recognize a zed head when I see one!"

"Whatever." I squinted out the window but still didn't see anything useful.

"We've got to finish him off," Jonah muttered. I stared at him in disbelief, but he didn't even flinch. His face was drawn and serious. "If we leave him there, he might attack someone else."

I looked down at my leg. I really wanted to tell him I was hurt too badly and he'd have to do it without me. But he'd saved my life. Twice. I couldn't wimp out on him now.

"You're going to have to help me pop my knee back into place," I said. "I can't run like this."

"Just tell me what to do."

I levered my body around, lifting my injured limb and setting it in his lap. It slanted sickeningly to the right. If it had been someone else's leg, I'd have been ooohing appreciatively, but I didn't even want to look at it. I wrapped my fingers around the armrest and held on as tightly as I could.

"Pull it straight out," I said. "Hard and fast."

"Isn't that going to hurt?"

"Do it!" I shouted, and he yanked hard on my leg before the words were even out. The pain was immense; I couldn't help but shriek. Little white stars danced across my field of vision. Sweat beaded on my upper lip, like I didn't look icky enough already with the mud coating and all.

"You okay?" Jonah asked.

I didn't trust myself to speak, so I nodded and tested the knee. It felt like it was back in place and seemed like it would bear my weight, although I wouldn't want to run a marathon or anything.

"All right." Jonah took a deep breath. "I want you to stay behind me, and if I get in trouble, you go for the car and run him over again, okay?"

"What are you going to do?"

He reached into the backseat and produced his pseudosword. It only took a minute to rip all the stupid foam off, leaving a long length of sturdy PVC. He thunked it into his hand. I tried to imagine it smashing into Coach's skull but quickly decided I didn't need the mental picture.

"I'm going to go hunt some zombie," he said. It would have sounded pretty cool if his voice hadn't cracked in the middle of the sentence.

He got out of the car. The last thing I wanted was to follow him, but I did anyway. I limped forward just far enough to get a good line of sight, but not so far that I couldn't lurch to the car in the event that zombies tried to flank me. They usually travel in numbers, assuming that Hollywood has it right.

Jonah shouldered the sword and inched toward the ditch. The closer he got, the more erratically my heart pounded. I started glancing around with barely suppressed paranoia. I'd seen enough horror movies to know that the zombie hordes always came from out of nowhere to descend on the girl when the guy's back was turned. They weren't going to sneak up on me, though.

Jonah leaned over the edge of the ditch, and I nearly jumped out of my skin, I was so scared. I couldn't keep from snapping at him.

"Jonah? Have you gone completely mental? If you go down there, you're on your own."

"I don't see him," he said, poking around in the underbrush with his sword. "I don't know where he could have gone."

"Probably in that big drainage pipe that goes under the road. And you're not going in there." I realized I was still cradling the foot under my arm. There were so many stray body parts around these days that I'd begun to feel pretty nonchalant about them. Either that or I was in shock. "Don't you remember when the Ludwigs' dog got stuck down there and the fire department had to get him out? There's no room to move, and definitely no room to swing at him. He'd tear you apart! Frankly, I'm surprised he fit in the first place."

Disappointed, Jonah lowered the sword.

"If he's in there," I continued, "we're not getting him out without a forklift. Let's go home. I want to take some pain meds and get cleaned up."

He nodded. "I'm sorry." He shouldered the sword again and offered his arm for me to lean on. He must have been in shock too, because the sight of the foot didn't faze him either. He just said, "You want me to carry that?"

"Nah. I've got it. I'm getting used to dismembered body parts."

He laughed, but I didn't understand what was so funny. I was being entirely serious.

CHAPTER twelve

I could see the glow of our house all the way from the end of the block. "Dad would flip if he saw that you left all the lights on," I said. Leave it to me to be worried about energy conservation at a time like this.

"I didn't." Jonah frowned like the lights were a personal affront. Like father, like son. Dad got a little crazy about green issues.

The front door opened before we could even get out of the car. Dad stepped outside and glowered at us so hard I felt the force of it from a hundred feet away.

"Katherine Curie and Jonah Salk Grable, get in the house right now," he said sternly.

I hobbled up the driveway under my father's stern gaze. Jonah hurried behind me and joined me inside on the couch. Dad didn't sit. He loomed over us in that parental way I thought they must teach in secret night classes. Then he folded his arms, as if we hadn't already gotten the picture that he was pissed.

"Someone," he said, "better start talking. Because otherwise, I will be forced to conclude the worst."

Confessions were the best way to avoid being punished, but I wasn't sure where to begin. "About what?" I asked.

He looked at me like I was a complete moron. "Perhaps it wasn't clear what I meant when I took your keys away. I meant that the car wasn't to be driven. Particularly by Jonah after dark on a school night, when the only licensed driver in the car might start convulsing any minute. What were you two thinking?"

"It was an emergency," I said, and I would have continued if Jonah hadn't butted in.

"Yeah, Kate had another seizure at school, and she needed a ride home. It's not like we ran anyone over or anything."

He was lucky Dad was there, or else I would have punched him. The last thing we needed was to inspire Dad to check out the front bumper and discover Coach's face imprinted on it. Luckily, Dad was focused on the driving itself, so the last sentence didn't register.

"So you decided to compound the problem by taking the car rather than calling me for help?" Dad asked. "I'm not impressed by your reasoning, Jonah."

"I was worried about her," Jonah said, mustering more sweetness than I thought possible. "So maybe I wasn't thinking clearly. I'm sorry."

Dad softened noticeably, uncrossing his arms and relaxing the ramrod-straight posture just a little. I'd have to ask Jonah to teach me that trick someday. I couldn't apologize without wanting to repeatedly whack my head on something.

Dad sighed. "Perhaps I'm overreacting. But if something had happened to you . . ."

"Everything's okay," I said. "I'm fine. Jonah's fine. The car is fine. And if something like this happens again, I'll call you at work, okay? I should have done that, but I wasn't exactly thinking clearly either."

He took a deep breath and ruffled my hair. "I'm sure you're upset at this sudden relapse, pumpkin. I can understand that. Just don't let it happen again, either of you. Okay?"

Jonah and I nodded like crazy.

"Good." Dad gave me a once-over. "Now go take a shower. It looks like you seized in the middle of a mud puddle."

"Oh." I looked down at my mud-spattered jeans and soaking wet socks and decided that the best explanation was no explanation at all. "Yeah. That's a good idea."

I felt much better once I took some painkillers and a shower. It amazed me how a stream of steaming water and some strawberry-scented shampoo could soothe the soul of the zombie-plagued.

The feeling didn't last long. I wrapped myself in my periodic-table robe and walked down the hall to my bedroom. My brother was hunched in front of my dresser, pawing through my underwear drawer. And for a minute I had actually started to like him.

"Jonah!" I shut the door behind me, because I didn't want Dad to overhear. He was on the alert already, and if I had to say the words "My brother touched my panties" aloud, I'd lose it. "What are you doing?"

He whirled around. My favorite panties, with I ♥ SCIENCE printed on the butt, fell out of his hand and onto his foot. I was never going to be able to wear them again.

"You stole my elf ear," he said, waving a pitiful piece of latex at me.

"What?"

"Ear thief. Anatomical kleptomaniac. Body-part pilferer."

"Oh yeah? Well, you happen to be wrong. I don't steal ears. I steal fing—"

I snapped my mouth shut.

"You steal what?" Jonah asked.

"Nothing." I muttered. "Get your hands off my underwear."

He put the ear in his pocket and slammed my dresser drawer shut. I knew it had been too good to last. He'd worn those stupid elf ears everywhere for an entire year; I'd had to take action before he started high school and I became known as the elf boy's older sister. Because really, I was geeky enough without my brother adding to it. The ear had been in the back of my underwear drawer for about four months. All my undies smelled like rubber, but it was a small price to pay for an elf-free reputation.

"You know what? I forgive you, even if it was a cruddy thing to do. I don't want to fight with you, Kate." He held his hands up, like an empty placating gesture was going to make up for the fact that his hands had just been on my underthings. "I was just looking for it."

"And you thought your ear might be inside your sister's underwear? You. Are. A. Freak."

"That's not what I'm talking about," he snapped.

"Well, if your pronoun had an antecedent, I might have some idea what you're talking about. And you're still a freak."

"You know exactly what I'm talking about," he said, edging closer to me. My panties slid off his foot. I was going to have to burn the contents of that entire drawer and buy all new underwear. "I was looking for the zombie foot. I thought maybe you'd put it in the dresser while you were in the shower. Where'd you hide it?"

"The foot? Oh crap!"

The delightful, relaxed postshower feeling evaporated immediately. We were back to full-on panic mode.

"Kate, you're killing me here." He folded his arms. "I want to know everything. How did you find out about the zombies? Did you know before we ran into Coach? His foot just fell off by itself, didn't it?" Then he let out some weird snort-cackle combo. "I totally can't believe my sister is a kick-butt zombie hunter. Wait till I tell the guys!"

"Jonah, you can't tell anyone I stole a foot," I hissed. "I'll get arrested."

"Yeah, I guess you're right." His face fell momentarily, but nothing was going to rain on his undead parade. "Well, can't I see the foot one more time? Come on. I didn't really get to look at it before."

I rubbed my head. "I think I left it downstairs. On the table. With Dad."

"You forgot the foot?" Jonah grabbed me by the shoulders and shook me, as if scrambling my brains was going to help anything. "How could you?"

"Jonah, I was attacked by zombies twice today. I had a seizure, and now I've got the beginnings of a monster migraine. So excuse me if I'm a little discombobulated." I couldn't believe I was justifying myself to my brother. "Like you were any better? You practically advertised the fact that we ran someone over with the car. Why not take him outside and offer to show him the skid marks while you're at it?"

He frowned. "Well, we can stand here and yell at each other until Dad finds the foot and decides we're grave robbers, or we can do something about it. When did you have the foot last?"

I thought back. After we got in the car, I'd wrapped the foot in a Country Kitchen grocery bag that was on the floor. I'd placed the bag on the coffee table while Dad was interrogating Jonah and me. I was almost sure of it.

The operative word there was *almost*. Normally I wouldn't

space out like that, but I was so tired. And hurt. And stressed. My brain was practically dribbling out my ears.

"All right," I said. "You check the car. There's a chance I left it in there. I'll check the living room, which is the other best possibility. Meet me in the basement."

"Okay."

Jonah thundered down the stairs.

The living room light was off and the room empty, which made my life easier. It would have been a lot more difficult to remove a foot-shaped bag from right under Dad's nose. I could probably have managed, but it was nice not to have to worry about it. I flicked the lights on with a feeling of relief.

The bag wasn't there.

I swallowed. It wasn't like the foot would walk off on its own. Or would it?

CHAPTER thirteen

I stared at the empty table and tried not to panic. The missing foot wasn't going to suddenly come to life and stomp my family to death, right? That kind of thing only happened in horror films, in which case I would have been a lot blonder and more buxom. It was one of the few situations in which my geekiness was reassuring.

The foot was probably in the car. I stared at the door to the garage, expecting Jonah to bound through triumphantly at any moment with a plastic bag full of foot. It didn't happen.

I heard Dad pounding away at the keyboard in his study down the hall, Armstrong growling as he worked on his nightly rawhide chewie. Personally, I could think of better things to do than sit on Dad's smelly feet and chew rawhide, but it was Armstrong's favorite activity in the world. He was really going at it tonight too. The snarly noises he made were almost comical.

Then it hit me. Oh my god. Armstrong had the foot.

All of Dad's work stuff had been on the table too. He'd probably grabbed the bag by mistake, and Armstrong got hold of the dismembered body part somehow, and now he was chewing it into bits.

I ran down to the study. Dad looked up from the computer with an expression of mild puzzlement.

"What?" he said, pushing his glasses up onto his nose. "Is there a fire?"

"No. I . . ." I looked around wildly. "Um. I forgot to take Armstrong out for a walk. Is he in here?"

Dad glanced at his dog-covered feet. I needed to distract him before he discovered what Armstrong was really chewing on.

"Dad!" He jerked at my shout. "Sorry. I just don't want to disturb you. And I know Mom would be upset if she came back from her trip overseas to find the carpet all yucked up."

Dad looked at me like I was insane. And really, I doubted Mom would notice if I dug up the living room and installed a swimming pool, even if she wasn't overseas. There was a reason we had a cleaning lady come once a week.

"Well, if it means that much to you, I'm not going to discourage you from performing your chores," he said, but he was watching me now. My erratic behavior had definitely gotten his attention. At this rate, I'd be lucky if he didn't decide to get me drug-tested.

I chuckled. It sounded so fakey stupid, but Dad was already back at the keyboard poundage and didn't seem to notice. I stooped down to reach under the desk and extract the zombie part from our dog's mouth. Once I got my hands on that foot, I was going to brush Armstrong's teeth about twenty times. He was a face licker, and I couldn't even think about that without wanting to throw up.

Armstrong was curled around his treat. I'd have to drag him out from under the desk to get the foot. I grabbed his foreleg and tugged, and he growled at me.

"Hey, Army," I cooed. "You want a walk? You can have your treat after we come back in."

He went back to chewing.

"I think he wants to be left alone, Kate," Dad said.

"Yeah, but I need to take him out."

"In your robe?" He arched a brow. "You're not making any sense, Kate."

"Well, I'll get dressed again," I replied somewhat desperately.

This wasn't going well. I pulled the periodic-table robe more tightly around myself, grabbed the dog, and tugged. He bit me. Not really hard, because he wasn't that kind of dog, but enough of a nip that it drew some blood. I yelped and withdrew my hand.

"Armstrong, bad!" Dad exclaimed, rolling up a piece of paper and tapping the dog on the hind end with it. I was surprised when he reached across the desk and biffed me on the head too. I put my hand to my scalp like the paper might have damaged me. "And you should know better, Kate. I told you he didn't want to be disturbed."

"Sorry," I said, but my attention was on Armstrong. He picked up a huge piece of rawhide shaped like an egg roll, gave me a reproachful glance, and walked out into the hall. I gaped at him for a minute before stooping to look under the desk. There was no sign of the foot. Just a couple of scattered bits of dog chew.

After a quick meltdown in the bathroom, I went downstairs. When I turned the corner at the bottom of the basement steps, Jonah leapt at me, waving a plastic bag in my face.

I'd never been so happy to see a Country Market bag in my life.

"It's a foot! A foot!" He kept waving the bag around like he was the newest member of the flag corp. My unnatural fraternal tolerance quickly wore off. I snatched the bag away and barely restrained myself from hitting him with it.

"Enough! It's a foot. I get it. Now give it to me so I can hide it in my underwear drawer before we get arrested for possession of dismembered body parts."

"You're no fun." He sulked.

"I don't have time for fun. I've got to prove there's a communicable disease that makes people act like zombies and figure out how it's spreading before everyone's infected. So you'll have to excuse me for not capering around like an idiot, okay?"

"Okay." He sat down in his computer chair, looking up at me from under a fringe of overlong hair. I would have been more inclined to take him seriously if he didn't look like such a wimpy emo-geek hybrid. And the fifteen empty cans of Mountain Dew that ringed his keyboard didn't exactly contribute to an air of responsibility. "What can I do?"

"Nothing, Jonah."

"That's no fair! You never let me have any fun, and I saved your butt today. Twice! I deserve—"

"Wait a minute." I held up a hand. "There is something you can do. If you're interested."

"What? I'll do anything." He was so excited he practically panted.

"Say I wanted to hack into a teacher's computer. Could you do that?"

"Are you kidding? I hacked into the duct-tape guy's Roargan Kross account and stole his Ring of Righteous Kills out from under his nose. I can get into anything. Are you talking a remote hack, or do you have physical access to the hard drive?"

"Well, I don't exactly have it in my pocket. I guess we could wait until tomorrow morning if we had to, but I'd rather not. Could you do it from here?"

"If it was important enough."

"You've seen what's at stake." I paused. I was pretty sure he'd do it, but I couldn't resist adding a little extra incentive. "If Kiki isn't infected yet, she probably will be soon. It's spreading fast."

The thought of a footless Kiki was too much for Jonah to bear. "You can count on me," he said. His voice cracked midsentence. It actually made me feel better. He sounded like a total computer geek, and that was exactly what I needed.

"Good," I said. "Coach gave some of the varsity players injections from a bunch of unmarked vials, and I think that's how the infection started. I need to know where he got those vials. I'm trying to put a packet of information together to send to Dr. Ho tomorrow, and this is a really important piece of the puzzle. Get what I mean?"

"Gotcha. So this information is stored on his computer at school?"

"I hope so. But I don't know for sure."

"Well, we'll never know until we look, will we?" He cracked his knuckles one by one; the sound made me wince. I hated it when he did that.

"Anything I can do to help?" I asked.

"Dew me. I'm going to need a serious caffeine buzz if I'm going to stay awake, and I don't know how long this'll take."

"I think there's a six-pack in the fridge. I'll get it. And if you want, I'll stay up with you," I offered, heading for the stairs.

"Don't bother. You'll only distract me." He looked up from the computer screen and grinned. "Besides, you need to rest your zombie-kicking butt. If this thing is spreading as fast as you say it is, we might have an interesting trip to school tomorrow."

After that comment, it took me forever to fall asleep. I spent hours lying in bed awake, trying to mathematically predict the spread of a zombie epidemic. It didn't bode well for the human race or for my sleep schedule.

CHAPTER fourteen

I forgot to set my alarm, but I was such an overachiever that I woke myself up without it. I knew I should brush my teeth first, but I couldn't restrain my curiosity. I went down the hall and tapped on Jonah's door. No answer. The bed was empty when I opened the door. I told myself firmly that there was no need to panic, because geekboy had fallen asleep at the computer before, but my stomach still twisted with nerves as I went downstairs.

He was snoozing on the keyboard. It was tempting to snap a picture, but I was too tired to go upstairs for the camera.

"Jonah, wake up," I said, shaking his shoulder.

"Wha—?" He lifted his head and looked at me with bleary eyes.

"Did you find anything?"

He rubbed his eyes and said something that might have been English.

"We don't have time for this. Go take a shower. I'll put some coffee on. You can brief me at the bus stop." I glanced at the clock hanging near the stairs. "I don't want to be late."

"Yeah. Okay."

I made it outside first. It was cold, drizzly, and still dark, which did wonders for my nerves. I huddled next to the garage door, because it was the best chance I had of not freezing my butt off, and as an added bonus it was a good way to keep zombies from sneaking up on me. The neighborhood seemed abnormally quiet this morning. Usually I could hear dogs barking and kids on their way to school and stuff. I kept telling myself it was just because of the icy rain, but I didn't really believe myself because I was a crappy liar.

Jonah walked out with his sword.

"There's no way the driver's going to let you on the bus with that thing."

"Yeah, I thought of that," he said. "I'm telling her it's—"

He broke off abruptly, dropped the sword, and dashed to the bushes alongside the garage. I heard the unmistakable sound of puking. I was becoming quite the expert on it.

When he straightened up and wiped black, ropy smears of saliva from his chin, it shook me so badly I forgot to breathe. I had assumed he was out of danger since everyone else I knew who'd been exposed was already exhibiting symptoms. Maybe it took longer if you contracted the disease by puke instead of by bite. As if that made it okay that my little brother was infected.

From the horrified look on his face, Jonah knew what this meant. I was glad I wouldn't have to tell him. I didn't think I could.

"Maybe you should go back inside," I whispered.

"No." He picked up the sword and brandished it defiantly, like maybe the virus would manifest in midair so he could whack it.

"But—" I reached a hand out to him.

"No!" He shoved me away and threw the sword. It spun through the air, hitting the side of the garage about two inches from my head. By the time I regained my balance, he was already halfway across the yard.

"Jonah, wait!"

"I'm dangerous," he panted. "Stay . . . away."

He leapt the hedge and sprinted around the side of the house. I heard the crash of his footsteps through the overgrown vegetable garden and the roar of the bus as it shifted gears at the bottom of the hill. It would be here in a minute.

I started to follow him automatically, because when had I ever done anything Jonah told me to? I was his older sister, which pretty much meant that when he gave me an order, I was contractually obligated to do the exact opposite. But I stopped after only a few steps.

He was right. Sure, I could take him in a fight if he lost

control; I had about five inches and fifteen pounds on him. But that didn't mean I should chase him. The best thing I could do for him and all the other infected was prove the existence of a virus, and that meant going to school and checking my lab results.

The bus hissed to a stop at the end of our driveway. I grabbed Jonah's backpack off the ground and jogged toward the street, scanning the bushes the entire way.

The sound of some obnoxious eighties tune blared out the open bus door. I climbed the steps and looked for an empty seat. I was the only upperclassman who still rode the stupid thing, so you would have thought I'd have the right to claim a good spot. But in the skewed world of our suburban high school, brain-dead freshman jock outranked senior biology goddess. I just hoped that the whole brain-dead part wasn't literal, because the only empty spot was directly across from one of the JV linebackers. If he was infected, I was in trouble. His pectoral muscles were about the size of Hawaii.

I sat down, watching Hawaii carefully in case he decided to attack. He smiled at me, but I'd learned my lesson. One minute they were sitting pretty; the next they were trying to bite your kneecaps off.

Jonah didn't like it when I went through his things, but under these circumstances he'd just have to deal. I was hoping to find some evidence, and I wasn't disappointed: inside his backpack were a few papers with my name scrawled across them.

It was a short stack of email printouts. The first one said:

```
To: hbrzeszczak@bayview.k12.oh.edu
From: sswan@bayview.k12.oh.edu

Hank,

I saw the game last night against Lakeway.
Sorry you're having such a tough time! Think
you'd be interested in the new performance
enhancer I've been developing? I'm calling
it Playwell, and it's made to solve problems
like yours. In lab tests on mice, Playwell
significantly increased endurance and pain
tolerance, which could give you the edge you
need to win a game this season. I've noted some
slight increases in aggression as well. What
do you have to lose . . . other than another
season's worth of games and the respect of
your fellow coaches? Let me know.

Best, Siobhan Swan
```

I felt like I'd been gut-punched. All those mice I'd worked on for her so-called government project . . . Had those been test subjects for this performance enhancer? The symptoms—aggression, endurance, pain tolerance—those things described the victims of the zombie virus. Had I helped infect all those people?

I flipped the page with shaking hands.

```
To: sswan@bayview.k12.oh.edu
From: hbrzeszczak@bayview.k12.oh.edu

Definitely interested. Mentioned it to a buddy
of mine who coaches rugby at the military
base. Do you have enough for him too?

Hank
```

A couple of brief emails arranged and confirmed a delivery time, nothing very interesting. But then Coach balked.

```
To: sswan@bayview.k12.oh.edu
From: hbrzeszczak@bayview.k12.oh.edu

Swannie, not sure I should be giving my boys
this stuff without testing it first. Took a dose
this morning. If I don't notice any side ef-
fects by tomorrow, I'll do the linebackers be-
fore homecoming. I'll need a replacement vial
for the one I used. Drop it in my mailbox?

Hank
```

And then there was another email from Coach. Based on the date, he could have sent it while we were at the bonfire. By that time, he knew something was wrong. I was willing to bet that was when he tore up his office, although I didn't know for sure. The email read:

```
To: sswan@bayview.k12.oh.edu
From: hbrzeszczak@bayview.k12.oh.edu

Swannie, got to talk. There's a problem.
Call me.
```

But Swannie didn't respond, or Jonah didn't print it, or maybe she called like he asked. But I bet she didn't. She was probably too busy carting all the evidence away in that big box I saw her taking out of the lab.

"How stupid am I?" I muttered, staring out the bus window. I should have known something was up; she wouldn't even let me touch the freaking thing. And I was so blinded by my whole scientist hero-worship thing that I didn't even think twice.

When the bus pulled to a stop in the loop outside the school, I launched myself out of the seat. Hawaii got up too. "Move!" I squeezed past him and stalked down the aisle.

For the first time in the known history of the universe, everyone shrank back in their seats to let the geek go first.

CHAPTER fifteen

Our bus was always ungodly early, so the chem lab was dark and empty when I arrived. Sunbeams trickled in through the frosted glass windows, and the lab equipment made twisted shadows on the floor. I didn't dare turn on the lights. I didn't want to scare Swannie off if she was here.

I was halfway through the main lab when Swannie's door opened and I saw a huge backlit Afro before the light clicked off. She was standing with her back to me, fiddling around with the locks. "Going somewhere?" I said, like a character from a TV movie.

She let out a little shriek and dropped something on her foot.

"Kate!" She put a hand to her chest. "Oh my god. You scared me."

"Whoops."

"What's up? I didn't expect to see you this morning."

"I wanted to check on my cultures." I looked from the brown paper bag on the floor to the guilty look on her face. She'd taken them. I knew it. "You haven't seen them, have you?"

"Um," she said, her free hand reaching up to toy nervously with her necklace. "No, I didn't notice any cultures. Are you sure you ran some?"

"Yeah, I'm sure. So what's in the bag?"

"Nothing! I mean, lunch. Nothing important."

"Ah." I nodded. "Did you buy lunch using the money you made on Playwell?"

"I'm not making any money on it!" She clapped a hand to her mouth, but it was too late. We both knew I had her.

"It's making people sick, Swannie. A lot of people."

"How do you know about Playwell?" she asked.

"Did you make it infective on purpose, or was that just a happy coincidence?" I asked, ignoring her question.

"In—infective?" she stammered. "What do you mean?"

"Oh, you know exactly what I mean. My brother's infected now, and it's all because of you. And you made me a part of it. That's the worst thing of all; part of this is my fault! All that mouse work you gave me was really a bunch of illegal drug testing!" I shouted. "I was so flattered that you'd let me help that I didn't even stop to question why you have all this stuff in a high school lab. I didn't think to ask what you were doing because I trusted you. How could you do that to me?"

Swannie had grown very pale. "I'm sorry, Kate. I—"

"Bull. If you really cared, you'd be trying to fix things instead of covering your butt. You took my cultures, didn't you? You'd better give them back before I take them from you by force."

I wasn't a violent person, but I meant what I said. I didn't understand how she could do something like this. She had been my idol—and she'd totally let me down.

"I didn't mean for this to happen," she said. "I just needed to make a little money. It's hard to get by on a teacher's salary. You've got to believe me, Kate. That's why I took all those research materials home. I've been trying to find a cure."

"Didn't you think maybe you should tell someone in the meantime? Even an anonymous tip is better than nothing. Because otherwise, it's just going to spread. Everyone is going to turn into a zombie eventually if we don't do something. But you're too worried about yourself to think of anything else, aren't you?"

She flinched. "It was just supposed to be a performance enhancer. I wasn't trying to hurt anybody." Then she hesitated. "Kate . . . we could work together to find a cure. In fact, we could maybe write a paper on it. A real paper, in a real science journal. We could put your name on it if you wanted."

It was a desperate bribe from a desperate person. But still . . . it made me pause. Sure, I was smart. I had great grades. But brainiac physician wannabes are a dime a dozen. If you want to get into the best pre-med programs, you have to be able to play concertos while blindfolded or spend your summers teaching sustainable farming to kids in Africa. I was determined to get into med school but partly afraid that I couldn't compete with people like that. But if I was the lead author on a scientific paper that described a new disease and its cure? I could choose any school I wanted.

And Swannie knew it.

She pressed her advantage, and the fact that I saw through it didn't make it any less effective. "You might be able to cure them. That's what I've been working on the past few days." She bit her lip. "Kate, I'll give you everything you need."

"Excuse me if I feel skeptical," I said. "Coach's foot fell off. How exactly do you propose to cure that? Superglue?"

She shook her head. "We need to concentrate on what we can cure. On the future, not the past. Based on my current data, this thing can be deadly if it's not treated. Neither of us wants that. The virus should respond to medication. It's just that I haven't quite identified the right drugs yet. Help me work on this and I'll make sure you're rewarded. We'll fix this together. No one has to know where it came from, right?"

It was so tempting. After all, I'd done all the legwork to develop Playwell in the first place; why shouldn't I share in the proceeds? Everyone would still be cured in the end. I wouldn't be hurting anyone else if I took her up on it.

"All right," I said reluctantly.

The look of relief on her face was instantaneous. Despite all efforts to the contrary, I couldn't help but pity her. All of a sudden, things had changed. I had always been desperate for her approval, and it had led me to do things I regretted. But now she was the desperate one.

"Thanks," Swannie blurted out, and for a moment I thought she might hug me. "I really appreciate you keeping this between us, Kate. It was an honest mistake. You know that, right?"

"Yeah," I said.

But there was no way I was going to keep this between us. It wasn't right, and the more I thought about the attempted bribe, the angrier I got. I'd play nice until I had enough evidence to turn her in. And then I'd write my own darned journal article. "Show me what you've got."

She smiled, relief in every line of her face. "Everything's in the bag. Why don't you take a look, and we can work on treatment possibilities after school tonight. I've got a few ideas already, and I'm sure you'll have some as well. I'd expect nothing less from you."

I peeked inside and saw printouts on the chemical breakdown of Playwell, along with a bunch of my data on the mouse testing. My work was meticulous and letter-perfect; it made me feel simultaneously proud and ashamed. I should have known. Legit high school teachers didn't do research like this, and they especially didn't let their students help. It was so blazingly obvious to me now; why hadn't I seen it before?

I pulled out my specimen dishes. I didn't even need a microscope to see the plaques on the culture that proved once and for all that those vials contained some kind of virus.

I had all the proof I needed. The Ho would listen to me now, assuming that I could get him to stop delivering babies and actually return my phone call.

My first instinct was to show the dish to Swannie. Old habits are hard to break. I held it up with a huge grin and said, "And there's our virus."

"Yep!" She beamed at me. "I'm so impressed that you figured it out. I'll have to make sure to mention your deductive skills in my letter of reference. I'll write you a great one for college."

I smiled.

It was going to feel so good to take her down.

I offered to set up our workstations, and Swannie was more than willing to let me do all the grunt work. But as soon as she left, I started arranging all the data on the worktables. I wanted photos for my records, and I figured I'd better send them to the Ho before Swannie made the evidence disappear.

I was about halfway done when the loudspeaker clicked on. The principal's disembodied voice filled the room. "Attention, all students. Please remember that we are on an abbreviated schedule today due to this afternoon's pep rally and announcement of the homecoming court. Thank you for getting to class on time."

I quickly labeled all the materials, snapped some pictures with my cell, and emailed them to the Ho's office. It only took a couple of minutes to tear it all down and stuff the labels into my backpack, where Swannie would never see them. And then I set up both workstations as rapidly as possible. I only had a few minutes left, but I'd set up these stations so many times I could have done it in my sleep.

As I walked to my locker, I saw Aaron leaning against it.

"Hey," I said.

"Hey." He scooted over a little so I could reach the lock, but he was still standing really close. Close enough that I had to try the locker door three times before the stupid thing opened.

"So did you get my text?" he asked.

Oh my god. After all the time I'd spent drooling over Aaron, you'd think I could remember to respond when he asked me to homecoming. Of course, the zombies needed to take priority, but I could have found two minutes to text him the word *yes*. Underlined. And with about six hundred exclamation points.

"I did." I smiled. "And I'd love to go with you. Sorry I didn't text you back. But the infection is spreading. I've been trying to figure out what it is." A zombie epidemic striking at the same time I get asked out by the boy of my dreams. Who would have thought?

"Oh, great," he said. "I mean, that sucks about the infection. But I'm happy about homecoming." He ran his fingers through his hair. "So it's spreading, huh? Have you notified the authorities about those vials? Because Mike can't even talk now. His mom was really flipping out when I called the house this morning. Couldn't get him on the cell, and I was worried. I tried to get her to take him to the doctor, but she's one of those new age people who think the medical industry is a huge secret conspiracy to give people autism."

We rolled our eyes in tandem, which was awesome.

"Well," I said, "I just picked up all the evidence a couple minutes ago and sent it to the Ho. There's a virus in those vials. I've got proof." And hopefully we'd have a cure and Jonah would be fine. At least, that was what I kept telling myself.

"What ho?"

"Oh. Dr. Ho. Naturally."

He grinned. "Naturally. Well, congrats. I'm honored to hang in the presence of such a genius."

"Quit making fun of me."

He held up his hands, laughing. "Who said I was?"

I didn't know how to answer, so I pulled out my bio and Latin books instead. Aaron took them from me before I could cram them into my backpack. It was really old-fashioned but still kind of sweet. "Thanks."

"No problem," he said. We started walking down the hall. I kept thinking I should tell him about Coach, but I didn't know how to bring it up. If someone had found him, we would have heard about it by now, wouldn't we? I thought maybe I should call 911 and give them an anonymous tip. But what if they traced the call? I couldn't do it. I couldn't risk being thrown in jail. Not now.

"I waited for you in the parking lot this morning. Did you sneak past me or something?"

"Nah. My car's been confiscated."

"Really? Why?"

"You know I have epilepsy, right?"

"Yeah, I saw you have a seizure once. No offense, but it was kind of freaky."

"Tell me about it. Anyway, I was in remission for a long time, and they let me get my license and everything. But then, a few days ago, I started having them again. My dad took my keys. Can't have me seizing all over the road, right?" I forced a laugh.

"That's weird." He shifted my books to his other hand so he could slide his arm around my shoulders. "Why do you think that happened?"

"No clue."

"Well, what were you doing when it happened the first time? Come on, Kate; you're a genius. It's part of your appeal."

"You're kidding, right?" I looked up at him through my bangs and tried not to go all giggly.

"Not." He steered me down the hallway, and people stopped to stare. For once, I kind of enjoyed the attention. "So what happened right before your first relapse seizure?"

I forced myself to stop smirking at the group of annoying, perky-voiced party girls who always insisted on standing in a herd right in front of my locker and never let me through. Today, they clustered by the water fountain and watched us with their mouths hanging open. I found it a definite improvement.

"Uh . . . let me think," I said, wrenching my mind back to the seizure thing. "It was the night of the bonfire. After I got home, I hit my head, fell down, and had a seizure."

He stopped, releasing my shoulder, and I was so out of it that I took another three or four steps without him before I realized it. I turned around. Aaron was all white and panicked-looking.

"What's wrong?" I asked.

"What you just said." Aaron stepped closer to me. "You had your first seizure right after"—he thumbed the slowly healing scab on my lip, and I flinched away from the contact—"this."

CHAPTER sixteen

We walked the rest of the way to bio in silence. I kept obsessively rubbing my finger over my lip lump, and Aaron was probably trying to figure out how he could get out of taking a walking disease vector with a lip crater to homecoming.

I stopped when we got to the door. The hallway had emptied fast; we only had a minute until the bell rang.

"Wait. I can't go in there," I said.

"Why not?" Aaron pulled his arm off my shoulders again. It had been nice while it lasted.

"What if Dr. Ho doesn't check his messages? I need to make sure he's taking care of things." I glanced into the classroom. Mrs. Mihalovic was setting up a bunch of stations and covering them with sterile blue sheets so no one could see what was under them, and I knew what that meant. It was pop quiz day. I was usually one of those freaks who wouldn't miss pop quiz day for the world, but today, I was a different kind of freak altogether. By the time this was all over, I'd probably be lucky if I wasn't the committed-to-an-insane-asylum kind of freak.

But this whole thing was my fault; I couldn't just sit around and wait for the Ho to show up and fix everything. Not if I wanted to live with myself. I could only think of one way to get out of the classroom so I could follow up with him, and I didn't like it. I would rather have stuck bamboo shards under my fingernails than done what I was about to do, but I was just going to have to swallow the embarrassment.

I threw myself on the floor.

I'd never seen myself seize, since I hadn't figured out the whole out-of-body experience thing yet. But I'd had it described to me plenty of times, so I figured I should be able to fake it pretty well. Most people panicked when they witnessed a seizure anyway. It wasn't like they were going to be critiquing my performance. So I shuddered and shook, and I felt like I was doing a great job until I managed to give myself a charley horse.

My fake seizure ended a lot more abruptly than I intended. I clenched my leg, trying not to cry. It hurt so bad. Aaron knelt down beside me and took my calf in his hands, smoothing out the spasming muscles with long, sure strokes of his thumbs.

"It's okay," he said, looking over my shoulder. I twisted my head to see the entire AP Biology class clustered in the doorway, staring at me like I'd grown a third eye. "She just strained a muscle during her seizure. Didn't you, Kate?"

He looked down at me and winked. I could put one over on a lot of people, including Mrs. Mihalovic, but Aaron was too smart, or maybe he just knew me too well already.

"Yeah," I said. "I'm okay now."

"Why don't you help her down to the nurse's office, Aaron?" Mrs. Mihalovic said. "And come back quickly, please. We're having a pop quiz today."

She closed the door, cutting off a chorus of moans from our classmates. I felt like moaning too. Maybe she'd let me take it later for fun.

We walked down the hall, nodding to a pair of freshmen sprinting for the door before Mr. Gilbert shut them out of freshman bio. "Care to explain what's going on?" Aaron asked once they were out of earshot.

"I had to fake it, Aaron. There are some things I haven't told you yet."

My heart pounded. He deserved to know about Mike's finger. The zombie virus. Coach. I felt bad for keeping everything from him this long. I hoped he wouldn't be too angry.

But when we turned the corner, a couple of the guidance counselors were standing in front of the nurse's office.

Mr. Wiesner, my counselor, nodded at me. "Kate," he said. "You're looking a little peaked."

"I was, uh, taking her to the nurse's office," Aaron said. "She had a seizure."

Mr. Wiesner clucked his tongue sympathetically and held the door open for me. I had no choice but to wave goodbye to Aaron while telepathically sending a thank-you for not proclaiming my fakeness in front of AP Bio and my fervent wish that he not get eaten by a zombie before homecoming.

"Thanks," I said as Aaron headed back to class. "I'll talk to you later."

Mrs. Rooney, the school nurse, and I had a long history together. I'd probably spent more time in her office than I had in homeroom. When I was an underclassman, she used to let me read her nursing books while I waited for Mom to pick me up after a particularly bad seizure.

"Kate," she said, frowning. "I haven't seen you here in a while."

"I had a seizure in Mrs. Mihalovic's class. I'm not feeling so good now."

"You look horrible, you poor thing."

It was almost insulting. I couldn't possibly look that bad. I almost started arguing with her over it before I realized that it would be awfully counterproductive.

"Shall I call your dad to come pick you up?" she asked.

"No!" She widened her eyes at me, and I forced myself to speak at a more reasonable volume. "He's in an important meeting today, and it was just a seizure. If I could just lie down in the back room for a little bit, I should be okay. I could probably even go back to bio in time to take our pop quiz."

She deposited me in the back room on her foldout cot with a glass of water and a thin blanket. I had my phone out about five seconds after she closed the door behind her. Dr. Ho's office number was still in my call history.

The phone barely rang before someone snatched it up and yelled, "What?"

"Uh . . ." I was kind of taken aback. Maybe there was a crossed line or something. I knew I hadn't dialed wrong. "I need to talk to Dr. Ho. Can you help me?"

"Afraid not, honey. Dr. Ho went rock climbing yesterday and fell off a cliff. I don't know when he'll be back in the office, but I imagine it'll be a while. Can I take a message?"

I started hyperventilating. It was nice to know that he wasn't avoiding me, but what was I supposed to do now? The Ho couldn't help cure zombies from traction. And really, if he was falling off cliffs, he wasn't as smart as I thought he was.

"Well?" she demanded.

"No message," I said.

She hung up on me. I wasn't very impressed with his secretarial staff. But I had a much bigger problem to worry about.

I eyed the door. I knew Mrs. Rooney worked with the health

department sometimes. If I could convince her that I wasn't completely batty, she could put me in touch with the right person. It was just a matter of constructing an airtight argument.

I lay there in the dark for a while, going through all the evidence in my head, thinking through the arguments she'd likely make and planning my responses. I had to be completely rational if I wanted her to listen to me, so I had to eliminate the Z-word from my vocabulary. Otherwise, she'd write me off as a total nutcase.

Finally, I flung open the door, ready to impress Mrs. Rooney with my viral detection abilities. It figured; she wasn't at her desk. I couldn't catch a break. But the secretaries liked me. Maybe one of them would page her if I asked nicely enough.

I was halfway to the administrative offices when the screaming started. I wasn't surprised. I'd known it was only a matter of time before the zombies started attacking.

I jogged toward the ruckus. I didn't hear anyone yelling "Zombies!" just yet; they seemed to be in the wordless panic-at-the-top-of-your-lungs stage. The noise came from the direction of the cafeteria, and I had horrific mental images of zombie lunch ladies. Our lunch ladies were kind of scary to begin with. But zombie lunch ladies? Almost as scary as clowns.

As I got closer, the screams grew so loud and shrill that I started to wish for earplugs. I turned down the hallway leading to the kitchen, and Mindi Skibinski came running in the other direction. She knocked me off my feet. Seriously, she could teach our linebackers something; I flew backward so fast that I slid across the lineolum on my butt and banged my head into the lockers. She didn't even pause. She was too busy running and screaming.

Only an idiot would walk in on a zombie infestation empty-handed, so I looked around for something to defend myself with. I entered the little alcove outside the kitchen, which was fitted with coat hooks and stocked with about a thousand hairnets. Nothing that would be vaguely useful in a zombie fight. It was almost enough to make me wish I was one of Jonah's geeky gamer friends; at least then I'd have a pseudosword.

I opened the door, letting out a blast of screaming that assaulted my eardrums, and then I dashed inside because I figured it might give me a slight edge of surprise. I was about to go into a room full of zombies armed only with a backpack. I'd take anything that could make me feel better about the situation.

The kitchen was crowded and steamy and always smelled like fish sticks no matter what they were cooking. I took two steps in and grabbed a pair of metal tongs, then inched around the storage freezer and into the main room.

"Ahhhh! Ahhhh!" One of the lunch ladies was crouched on her hands and knees atop the metal counter, screaming at the top of her lungs. When she saw me, she pointed at the floor and screamed some more, like maybe I hadn't gotten the picture yet. I looked down at my feet, expecting to see a sneaky ninja zombie.

Instead, a bug crawled over the toe of my shoe.

But the word *bug* didn't quite do it justice. This was no mere insect; it was a strange mutant creature the length of my index finger, and I swore I could feel its weight as it skittled over my foot.

"Ewww!" I made a loud noise that sounded suspiciously like a scream and kicked my leg wildly. The offending creature sailed through the air, narrowly missing one of the other lunch ladies, who screamed at me and waved her hands around like the airflow might deflect any other airborne insects.

Okay. These were freakishly big bugs, but still? They were *bugs*.

Another one crawled out from underneath the sink; it looked like some kind of roach. Nothing to be afraid of; it wasn't like we were talking brown recluse spiders or something else poisonous.

I'd had enough of the screaming. I grabbed the nearest lunch lady by the shoulders and shook her. "Stop shouting! It's just a roach!"

She stopped midshriek, but her face stayed scrunched up like she was still screaming and I had merely managed to mute her with my mind. It was a superpower I had often wished for but had never managed to make work.

"They hiss," she said. "I'm getting out of here." She walked out the door, and the rest of the lunch ladies followed, muttering angrily.

I searched the kitchen. No zombies, but those freaky bugs were everywhere.

I decided to swing through the cafeteria. I let myself through the doors and walked right into a big herd of jerseyed JV football players standing in a big semicircle with their backs to me.

"Dude!" said one of them. They were all taking pictures of the bugs with their cell phones and punching each other on the shoulders. Just another moment when I realized how little I understood about guys.

I knew I should sneak out before they saw me, because this was clearly not a nerd-friendly situation. But today I wasn't in the mood to retreat.

"Hey, you guys know what's up with the bugs?" I asked.

They squinted at me like I was speaking Swahili. Then they turned back to what they were doing. Again, another hint that I should just leave, but I was tired of backing down. I'd talked to Aaron when I thought I couldn't. I could do this too.

"Hey! Do any of you know what's up with all the bugs?" I said it a little louder this time.

They turned around again, in perfect unison, like maybe they practiced synchronized turning in their spare time.

"You talking to us?" said a guy with short dark hair and a black T-shirt, stepping forward and shoving his chest at me. It wasn't as impressive as Hawaii's.

On a normal day, I would have gone all meek and inoffensive, as dictated by my geek survival instincts. But not today.

"Yes," I said patiently. "There's no one else here."

He didn't quite know what to make of me. He looked back at his friends like maybe they'd give him a clue on how to handle the geek. They didn't.

That's when I noticed the injection mark peeking out from

the sleeve of his T-shirt. I grabbed his arm in an attempt to get a closer look, but I would have had better luck moving the Great Wall of China with my pinky finger. He shoved me away, glowering, and raised his fists. He thought I was trying to pick a fight with him.

"Did Coach inject you with something?" I rattled the question off quickly, before he could pound my teeth in. The thug paused, his brow furrowing.

"Huh?" he asked.

"Did Coach give you a shot?" I spoke slower this time, pointing to the mark on his arm.

"What's it to you?"

"Look." I took his arm gently and lifted his sleeve to expose the circular bruise on his arm. "Coach was giving out some B twelve, and it's tainted. So he asked me to get all of it back. Do you have any?"

He squinted at me uncertainly.

"I think you should give it to her," said a deep voice from behind me. I turned around to see Hawaii. "This chick's pretty cool."

"Thanks," I said, surprised. "So he did give you some? How many of you used it?"

They all just stared at me, and I was starting to get a little impatient. I'd never seen many benefits to popularity, but I was beginning to understand its uses. If I'd been Kiki, I'd have had them eating out of my hand already instead of staring at me like I was one of those stupid bugs.

I looked up at Hawaii. "Well?"

"Ray's the only one who used it." He shuffled from foot to foot. "I don't like needles."

"Ray?" I asked, turning to the black T-shirt guy. "Have you been puking?"

He shook his head. Now he was starting to look scared.

"Good." I kept my voice low and soothing. "I'm going to find some medicine that will take care of things, and I'll make sure you get some. Can I have all the doses you've got left? We need to make sure no one else uses them."

Ray rummaged in his pocket and handed me a plastic bag full of vials. "Here," he said. "Coach isn't here today. Guess he called in sick or something."

I blinked. "Yeah. Well. Can you make sure none of the other JV guys have any of this stuff? It really is dangerous."

Hawaii nodded. I was about to leave when curiosity got the better of me.

"So what's with the bugs?" I asked.

"JV homecoming week prank," Hawaii said. "We let a thousand hissing cockroaches loose in the kitchen. Ray's uncle owns a pet store." I rolled my eyes, and he shrugged uncomfortably. "Hey, it's a tradition."

"Yeah, but couldn't you come up with anything better than bugs in the cafeteria? That's weak, guys. Very weak."

"We also duct-taped Mr. Gnepper in his office," Ray said proudly.

Well, that explained the lack of hall-monitor response to the screaming.

"Wow. Impressive," I said, shaking my head.

Hawaii blushed and shuffled his feet. "Not really. Listen, can I ask you a question?"

"Sure."

I expected a zombie-related inquiry. I did not expect him to pull me to the far end of the cafeteria and say, "Would you . . . I mean, will you go to homecoming with me?"

"I'm sorry?"

"Is that a no?" The poor kid looked so miserable that I felt kind of guilty. He seemed like an okay guy, even if his pectorals were scary and he hung with a bunch of football jocks.

"No. I mean, yes." I smacked myself on the forehead. "No, what I mean is that it's nice of you to ask, but I already have a date."

"Man, that sucks," he muttered. "Who?"

"Aaron Kingsman."

Now he backed away from me, his hands flying up like Aaron's name had generated some kind of invisible force field. I was now untouchable. I patted him on the shoulder awkwardly and said, "Listen, I'd better go if I'm going to get that medicine." And then I tripped over his foot.

Hawaii caught me by the elbow and held on until he was sure I wasn't going to run face-first into the wall. Then he released me. I smiled at him, and he went scarlet. I didn't know how I'd suddenly morphed into a guy magnet, but I kind of liked it.

I grinned all the way out the door and back down the hall to-ward Mrs. Rooney's office. I was feeling pretty good until I had another seizure.

This time, at least no one witnessed it. The hall monitors were off inflicting demerits somewhere else today, with the exception of Mr. Gnepper, who was taped to a chair. No one noticed the girl against locker 1276 doing the neurological watusi. When it was over, I pushed myself into a sitting position against the wall and frowned at my knees like they'd done something to offend me. The whole seizure thing was really ticking me off. And I didn't get why being bitten turned everyone else into undead wannabes, but all I got was complete epileptic relapse.

On top of everything else, I'd forgotten to inject my seizure meds this morning. Good thing I had an emergency supply in Mrs. Rooney's office. I picked myself up off the floor and went back into her office. Her chair was still empty; I would have been offended at her lack of concern for my safety, but it was kind of flattering that she didn't feel the need to hover over my shoulder.

The med cabinet was locked, but I knew where she kept the spare key. Her trust in me must have been misplaced, because I opened the door and administered my meds without supervision, which was totally against school rules. I didn't even know why I bothered, since the meds were obviously useless. If anything, my seizures were worse than ever.

That was when it hit me.

My meds *were* still working. The injections were keeping me from turning into a zombie. It was the only logical explanation. If I was right, I could cure the virus. I wouldn't need to waste time convincing Mrs. Rooney, and then convincing the people at the health department, and so on. I could cure it and then let them take their time making up their minds whether to believe me. Because by the time they decided to take action, half the student body would be missing half their bodies. I could develop the cure myself and then take it, along with all the evidence implicating Swannie, to the health department. Things would go much more quickly that way.

I snatched all four of the doses left in Mrs. Rooney's stock. I figured it should be enough to test the cure; I could stop at home for more if it worked. Now all I needed was to administer it. Sure, I could try one of the guys on the team, but it wouldn't look good if I blasted into a classroom and started randomly injecting people. And I wanted to make sure it was safe before I tried it on Jonah.

I needed a test zombie.

And I knew just where to find one.

CHAPTER seventeen

I felt pretty guilty rifling through Mrs. Rooney's desk *again*, but not guilty enough to stop. I had a good reason. Heck, I had identified a potential cure while the rest of the medical world didn't even know there was a virus. That excused just about anything.

I flipped through a few files before I found the right section. Every student with a prescription medication needed to provide authorization paperwork, and I was betting Mike had an EpiPen in Mrs. Rooney's office as well as in Coach's. I hoped his home address was somewhere in that paperwork.

I'd been to his house a few times. He lived on a farm way outside the city limits; his mom had let the school use her barn for the annual haunted house fund-raiser. Too bad I couldn't remember where it was.

Bingo. There was his address. I used Mrs. Rooney's computer to get directions.

On my way out the door again, I ran into Mrs. Rooney.

"Are you okay?" she asked. "I'm sorry to leave you alone so long. I think the flu's going around again."

"I'm fine," I said, barely slowing down. "Gotta get to class in time to take that quiz!"

I was lying, of course. I really had to find Rocky and convince her to skip class with me.

She wasn't at her locker, but I saw her going into the girls' room down the hall. I slipped into the bathroom and up to the first stall door.

"Rocky? It's me. Kate. I have to talk to you."

"Um, Kate?" Rocky's voice came from the stall at the end. "I'm down here."

I walked over just as she flounced out.

"Hey!" she said. "What's up?"

"You have to come with me to Mike's," I told her. "I have to inject him with my seizure medicine."

Rocky stared at me. "Kate, I know you don't like him, but—"

I shook my head. "You don't understand." I whispered a sixty-second summary of events into her ear.

"So you need to do it right now? I've got my solo audition for the Holiday Showcase next period," she said, slathering on lip gloss. "So let me put it this way. If I go with you, I'm going to have to explain to Juilliard why I wasn't featured in the winter show. Do you need me that badly, or could you just take my car?"

"Rocky, if I seize and drive it off the road—"

"Then don't seize. I trust you." The bell rang, and she detached her key ring from her backpack and tossed it at me. "I've got to go. I'll be sending you good injecting vibes, though."

I felt pretty bad for having forgotten about her audition, not to mention nervous about having to go to Mike's alone. I couldn't really blame her for not coming with me—but then again, if my cure didn't work, Rocky would probably have to explain to Juilliard why our entire school had turned into zombies.

Sneaking out of the building was easy. But it took me a good forty minutes to get to Mike's house, because I drove like an old lady. When I got there, I pulled Rocky's car into the driveway, which was basically at the bottom of a ravine, and parked.

Shaking like a leaf, I got out of the car and climbed the rickety porch steps.

"How the hell am I going to inject Mike Luzier without getting killed?" I whispered to myself, swallowing a huge lump of fear. Going alone to the home of my zombified linebacker ex was not the smartest thing I'd ever done. It didn't take a genius to realize he wasn't going to roll over and offer me his arm for injection.

"He's probably going to try and bite my lips off again," I added under my breath, attempting to prepare for the worst.

But Jonah needed the cure. And that was why I was standing on Mike's porch ringing his bell.

No answer. I checked the door, but it was locked. No movement as far as I could see inside the house, and there weren't any cars in the drive. Either Mike's mom had finally gotten over her fear of doctors and taken him to one, or she had left him alone and now he was dead.

I banged on the door and stabbed the bell so hard that my finger hurt. If he was dead, I was determined to pester him back to life. It didn't work, though. I looked around for a rock to throw through a window, but the door opened before I found one. It was very horror-film cliché of me, but I could only do one thing.

I screamed.

CHAPTER eighteen

Mike Luzier stood in the doorway. A piece of his scalp had ripped loose and was dangling to his shoulder. Blood dribbled from his mouth, and I wasn't sure whose it was. He wore his football uniform; his body looked totally misshapen underneath it. He moved toward me with an uncoordinated lurch.

I stumbled backward off his front porch, twisting my ankle and sprawling in the mud. My little zipper bag of syringes and medication vials fell from under my arm and plopped into a puddle. I grabbed it and held it to my chest like it might have secret zombie-repellent properties. That was when I realized I was still screaming.

Some detached part of my mind took stock of Mike's various injuries, but the rest of me was in flight mode. I scrambled for the car, but it wasn't parked in front of the garage where I'd left it. I hadn't put on the emergency brake, so it had slid back down the muddy slope of the driveway. No way was I running down into that mud pit with a zombie at my heels.

I sprinted across the yard instead, drenching my shoes and nearly falling twice. The barn loomed over me, a dark and creaky structure that only served to intensify my hysteria. I heard a clatter, followed by a pained moan as Mike fell down the porch steps.

I bolted the barn door behind me, which was great except now the barn was pitch-black and superspooky. I opened my phone and used the dim light from the display to find a light switch and flick it on. Big mistake.

The barn was suddenly awash in red light. The walls glistened like they were painted with blood.

"Ahhhh!" I screamed some more, and I wasn't the only one. The damp air filled with howls and wails, accompanied by a chorus of dramatic violins and screeching doors.

I shut my mouth abruptly, and the screaming and screeching in the background carried on through the speaker above my head.

The haunted house from the fund-raiser. The Luziers had left it up. This realization made me feel slightly better. Only slightly.

I got out a syringe and snapped a vial into place. The door rattled against my back as Mike threw himself against it. I gulped, trying to reassure myself that I wasn't scared witless. I'd pop the syringe into his thigh and be back out of range in a flash. It would be easy.

A little voice in my head asked if he was really worth curing. I could run for the car and get the hell out of here. Why should I risk myself for Mike Luzier, of all people?

But I needed to know if the injection worked. Besides, the stubborn part of me refused to abandon him. I couldn't leave him to die just because he was a tool. I'd had to do that with Coach, and once was enough.

I took a deep breath before opening the door, or trying to, anyway. I couldn't find the handle. Either it had fallen off or the Luziers had removed it on purpose, which totally ticked me off, and not just because it was a fire hazard. Peachy. The only way out was to go through the haunted house.

The entryway was enclosed by tall plywood walls on which were scrawled the words *Abandon hope, all ye who enter here*. Very original.

I squeezed through the narrow corridor leading into the maze, which was a little claustrophobia-inducing but otherwise okay. Slick plastic lining the passage reflected the red light and made the walls look like they were covered with blood but also made the squeezing part easier. When I turned the corner, my foot triggered a blast of cold air right in my face. I nearly jumped out of my skin. Still, livable. I could deal with air compressor attacks.

Moments later, a wall-mounted speaker let out a massive wail right in my face. The volume was cranked up so high it made my head throb. I started searching for an off switch and knocked the speaker off the wall by mistake. The screaming was now accompanied by a constant high-pitched whine from the damaged sound equipment.

I turned, and a grotesque figure leapt into my path. I lifted my syringe to strike as it loomed over me. It was bottom-heavy, bulbous. I realized what I was doing about five seconds before I stabbed my reflection in one of those fun-house mirrors. Talk about overreacting.

I was still berating myself when the clown jumped at me.

A dummy with a painted face sailed down its wire straight at my head, arms outstretched and teeth bared. His mouth was rimmed in red; it looked like blood. A voice from a speaker to my left started cackling maniacally; lights flashed in a staccato rhythm all around the narrow corridor. The clown shook from side to side. I knew it was fake, but I swore it was reaching for me.

I freaked out.

My syringe plunged into its eye. I yelled when I did it too, like I was in a martial arts movie. Or maybe I was screaming and hoped to make myself feel less like an idiot by calling it something else in my head. The clown, thankfully, was a dummy on a pole. It didn't mind being stabbed in the eye; it just kept shaking and cackling. I should probably have taken the syringe out, but I couldn't make myself approach the thing. I left it wobbling there to scare the crap out of the next person who walked this stupid maze. I still had a few doses left.

I moved forward cautiously instead, another syringe at the ready. Mike could have come in the other side, or there might be more clowns. But I managed to push open the door and emerged back into the misty gray yard without being accosted by anything icky-faced or dead.

I returned to the front of the house. No Mike. I saw the big divot in the ground where he'd fallen off the porch and an uneven line running past the barn door and into the trees, like he had dragged his twisted foot through the grass the whole way there. A big stretch of woods bordered the house. Mike's trail led inside.

I ran to the car. If I flashed the lights and honked the horn, it would attract Mike's attention. I could wait for him in the car and roll the window down to inject him from the safety of the interior.

It was a great plan. Unfortunately, when I pressed on the gas pedal, the car didn't go anywhere. I put it in reverse. Then I tried drive. The only result was a furious whir of tires and lots of mud flying around. I reluctantly got out to see what was wrong. The two rear tires were sunk in a mud pit.

My dad had prepared me for situations like this, because we were that kind of family. I kept a bunch of emergency materials in my trunk. So if this had been my car, I would have wrestled a big bag of sand out of the back. Or, more likely, I would have tried to pick it up, realized I was too big of a wuss, and carted the sand out one plastic cup at a time. But I would have gotten the car out one way or another.

Rocky, unfortunately, had a very different kind of family. Her trunk was full of unsold Girl Scout cookies.

I was stuck here. At least I had a year's supply of Thin Mints.

* * *

I considered my options. I couldn't call Rocky or Jonah for help, because it was smack in the middle of third period. I didn't really want to call Dad. And I couldn't drive anywhere.

I'd just have to go on a zombie hunt.

I decided to check the house first, just in case. The front door still stood wide open; I nudged it with my foot. Mike might have snuck back inside while I wasn't looking.

There were no zombies behind the door, or anywhere else in the living room, for that matter. But the place was a mess. A moldy plate of half-eaten food sat on the coffee table, bugs swarming over it. The floor was strewn with clothes, smelly shoes, and random bits of paper; the cushions hung half off the sofa. The TV blasted some random cooking show. Some chef was chopping carrots at the speed of light. I stabbed the power button and the screen went dark.

I didn't see the body slumped in the hallway until I tripped over it. I jumped back and held my hands up like I knew karate. I didn't, but the zombies didn't know that. The lump on the floor remained motionless, though. I edged forward, turning the light on to get a better look. I instantly regretted that.

I couldn't remember what Mike's mom looked like, but I assumed this was her. She looked really young. Maybe it was the dreadlocks.

She was slumped facedown in the corner, the dreads spread out around her head like rays of the sun in a preschooler's drawing. I was a little nervous about touching her, because maybe this was all a trap and she was going to try to bite off the part of my lip her son had missed. So I flipped her over and jumped back before I even got a good look at her.

The jump? Completely unnecessary. She was very dead. Her eyes bulged from their sockets, and her face was riddled with bite marks. I clamped my hands over my mouth and backed away. I couldn't bear to look at her again. There was nothing I could do for her now, and I was going to have nightmares as it was.

If Mike was going all cannibalistic, there was an awfully good chance the rest of the defensive line was doing the same or would be soon.

This did not bode well.

No way was I going to chase Mike through the woods now, not if he was a murderer. I needed another test subject. I still wasn't thrilled about the idea of using Jonah to test the cure, but it was a better choice than playing hide-and-seek in the woods with a killer.

I stepped over the body and walked into the linen closet by accident before I figured out which door led to the garage. And there was exactly what I needed.

Mike's 4x4, keys in the ignition.

CHAPTER nineteen

Forty minutes later, I swung into my driveway. I smacked the vials into the syringes with the practiced motion of a gunslinger in a bad Western and slipped them into my belt, one on either side. Then I stepped out of the SUV, squared my shoulders, and marched through my front door.

Or at least, I tried to.

It was locked, and I ended up fumbling around in the depths of my backpack. I couldn't find my keys. It completely ruined the mental picture I had of myself as an action heroine.

When I finally managed to get inside, the house was silent. I snuck down to the basement. The lights were off, but I wasn't willing to take it for granted that Jonah wasn't there. I crept down the stairs and swung around the corner at the bottom, a syringe held high. But there were no zombified little brothers in the basement. Normally, I would have been relieved by this, but under the circumstances I was disappointed.

I methodically worked my way through the first floor. No Jonah in the kitchen, living room, study, or dining room. He wasn't hiding in the downstairs bathroom. (No big surprise; that bathroom was tiny, but I checked it anyway to be thorough.) I went upstairs and crept down the hall to Jonah's bedroom door. It was barely cracked; I kicked it open with the heel of my foot and leapt inside, a syringe in each hand. The room was empty, except for about fifty dollars' worth of empty soda cans and enough dirty laundry to clothe our high school for a month.

"If I was Jonah, where would I go?" I mumbled, walking outside. I'd have to try to track him, although you could write what I knew about outdoorsy stuff on the back of a postage stamp and still have room left over. I started at the side of the house where we'd been waiting for the bus, followed the path of mass destruction through the garden, and emerged in the backyard.

Bang!

The loud noise scared me so badly that I tripped over one of the lawn chairs.

Bang!

I ducked behind the table. We didn't have a privacy fence, so our neighbors had a clear line of sight to our backyard. Maybe someone had seen Jonah; maybe he had attacked someone and now they were shooting at him. If that was the case, I couldn't afford to wait. I stood up and waved my arms.

"Stop!" I yelled. "Stop shooting. He's just sick. I can cure him!"

Bang! Bang!

This time, I caught movement out of the corner of my eye; I whirled in that direction. The shed door hung loose. As I watched, a burst of wind slammed it against the frame.

I sprinted for the shed. That door always stayed locked, because some idiot had taken our riding mower for a joyride one year and driven it into the lake down the street. There was only one person who could have unlocked it, and I was searching for him so I could stab him with a syringe.

I flung the door open. I was prepared for a lot of things: Jonah injured, Jonah aggressive, Jonah grunting in monosyllables. I was not prepared to find him duct-taped to a lawn chair.

Thick bands of silver wrapped around his torso, fastening it to the sturdy metal back. His hands were bound in his lap, his ankles to the legs of the chair. Strips of tape crisscrossed his mouth. He was whipping his body back and forth, but there was too much tape and it was stuck tight. The only way he was breaking out of this was if the ghost of Harry Houdini materialized out of the ether and possessed him.

When he saw me, his eyes bugged out.

"Uuuungh!" he grunted through the mouthful of tape.

"Jonah!" I exclaimed, ripping the tape from his mouth.

He lurched in my direction, straining against the tape. The chair tilted, slamming him to the floor. "Hungry!" he snarled, closing his jaws on my foot.

I should have been expecting this, but it still took me by surprise. I fell backward, nearly impaling my head on a rake. The fall put me face to face with him, an arrangement I immediately regretted. His eyes were empty of both reason and recognition. It frightened me more than anything else had so far; Jonah and I might have made each other's lives miserable, but we still had each other's backs and always would. Or at least, we always had before he'd gotten zombified.

Unfortunately, I'd dropped the syringes when I fell, and Jonah was about to ingest my big toe. I grabbed the only thing within reach: the rake. I flipped it around and used the handle as a prod— I just couldn't make myself rake my brother across the face. His teeth were sunk deep in my shoe. The situation reminded me uncomfortably of Coach.

I stretched out on the floor, groping around for the syringes. The door had swung shut, cutting off most of the light, so I was pretty much working blind. I couldn't feel anything. Jonah was light, but when you added a heavy metal lawn chair and about fifteen pounds of duct tape, it wasn't so easy to drag him around by one foot. I finally brushed one syringe with my finger and only managed to knock it farther away.

I swung the rake handle, aiming for my brother's shoulder. It slammed into the chair instead.

The good news? His teeth released my foot.

The bad news? I heard a loud rip as some of the tape gave way. I didn't even take the time to look; I leapt for the syringe, sprawling across the dirt floor on my stomach. My hands closed on it just as his weight settled on the back of my legs. His mouth clamped down on my calf.

Pain blazed up my leg. His teeth sank into my gastrocnemius muscle, and he shook his head like a dog with a bone. I had to get him off me. I bucked wildly, but his teeth were in deep and it only made the pain worse. I fumbled with the syringe, dropped it, and picked it up again with panic-clumsy fingers. Finally, I managed to pop the cap off. The needle easily pierced the flesh of his neck. I pushed down on the plunger and hoped the effect would be instantaneous.

It wasn't. Nothing happened.

Jonah started making this wet slurping noise as my blood burbled up and flowed out the sides of his mouth. I felt the flesh of my leg start to give with a wet rip that made my belly heave. The pain was huge. Tears ran down my cheeks.

Suddenly, Jonah released me. I took the opportunity to scramble backward and ran for the door, leaving the syringe still embedded in his neck. It wobbled as he flailed around, still half attached to the chair. I groped for the rake, holding it out in front of the open door in what was supposed to be a threatening manner.

Then he puked all over the side of the riding mower.

That puke was the most wonderful thing I'd ever seen. It

was green. And a little red. Technicolor, really, the color puke is supposed to be. It definitely wasn't black, and it didn't smell like toasty poop.

This was a good sign.

I grabbed the workbench and pulled myself to my feet with the rake in my hand and another syringe at the ready. I didn't know what dosage level he'd need to be completely cured. And really, I might have been immune to the virus because of my meds, but I wasn't immune to being mauled, as my calf would attest.

Eventually he stopped puking.

"Jonah?" I asked, my voice quavering.

"Quit pointing that thing at me," he said irritably.

Relief swam through me; I could have just about kissed him. "Are you okay?" I was feeling pretty hopeful, but I didn't lower the rake.

"My mouth tastes like someone brushed my teeth with a slab of rotten beef," he muttered.

Nice metaphor, bro. But I was so happy to have him back that all I said was "I'll take that as a big no."

He said something else then, but I missed it because I was too busy trying to count his breaths. If anything, his respiration was a little elevated. And his skin tone had warmed back up already; he no longer looked like he had a bad case of freezer burn.

"Kate?" He dragged the chair over to me. It made a horrible nails-on-the-chalkboard kind of sound. "You're not listening."

"Huh?"

"What happened?"

"I was hoping you'd tell me, Jonah. How did you get taped to that chair?"

"I did it myself, right after you left. Everything after that's a blur." He tried to wipe his mouth, but he couldn't quite reach. "Can you get me out of here?"

I lurched in his direction, trying not to move my injured leg. The pain had settled down to a dull, constant burn punctuated by flares of intense throbbing.

"What exactly compelled you to fasten yourself to a lawn chair?" I asked, trying to unstick him. I was getting nowhere quick, so I grabbed a pair of garden shears and tried to remove the tape without slicing his shirt to ribbons.

"I didn't want to hurt anyone, and I really felt like just . . . hurting someone. As soon as you left, I snuck in here and taped myself to the chair. It was the only thing I could think of. It worked too, although I probably should have gone to the bathroom first."

"How do you feel now?"

"Exhausted. And sick to my stomach. Not that I'm complaining," he added hastily. "I don't know what you gave me, but I feel a lot better now. Just exhausted. After a while, I started having problems thinking clearly. I don't really remember what happened after that."

I pulled the last bit of tape free. But when he tried to stand, his knees wobbled underneath him and he crumpled to the floor.

"I'm sorry." He hung his head. "I'm just so tired."

"It doesn't matter. Let's get you to bed."

We went to the house and lurched up the stairs together, and I deposited him in his room. After a brief stop to bandage my leg and pick up every last vial of seizure meds in the house, I was ready for action. Time to take my evidence to the health department. I didn't expect them to believe me, but I had to try. My only other choice was to take on the zombies all by myself.

And I really didn't want to do that.

CHAPTER
twenty

The waiting area at the health department was packed with children running around and screaming at the top of their lungs. Apparently they were holding a free flu clinic today, so I had to wait in a really long line before I could talk to anybody. In my tote bag were the seizure meds I had left. I'd only found twenty vials, which certainly wasn't enough to cure all the infected, but I figured the health department would be able to get more.

When I finally got up to the desk, I quickly and carefully unpacked my evidence: the cell cultures, the paperwork, and a vial of my medication.

The woman behind the desk pushed her glasses up on her nose. "Okay, what's all this?"

"There's a virus spreading through the population of Bayview High. I ran the cell culture from—"

"Put it all in this, please. I'll have someone take a look at it and get back to you." She smacked a manila envelope down on the table, followed by a Sharpie.

"But . . . this is urgent."

"I'm sure it is." She didn't sound unkind, just tired, and that actually made me feel worse. If she'd been rude, at least I could have blamed my failure on her. "I've also got water samples from a woman who is convinced that pesticides in her well gave her cancer. Yesterday, I got a deer we're supposed to test for chronic wasting disease, and earlier this morning, someone dropped off a bunch of tuna to test for salmonella. My whole office smells like fish. All these things are urgent. We will get to your materials, but we just can't drop everything and do it right now. As you can see, we're a little swamped."

I almost told her about Mrs. Luzier, but I decided against it. She'd have to call the police, and if things worked the way they did on TV, I'd be stuck in an interrogation room while Mike and the rest of the zombies ran rampant through town. I needed to stay free until I knew they had been cured.

"I'm sorry. I didn't think that through before I asked." I un-capped the Sharpie and quickly scribbled my name and cell number on the envelope. Then she tried to take it from me, but I held on tight and caught her eyes before she got away. "Listen, I realize it's a lot to ask, and I know you're incredibly busy, but do you think you could get someone to look at this today? A lot of my friends are sick, and . . . I'm scared. Can you help me?"

She gently tugged the package away. "You seem like a nice girl, so I'll do my best. But I can't make any promises."

When I got back to school, I slipped a note into Rocky's locker asking her to meet me before the pep rally, and then I headed for the locker room. Going to class now was only going to invite questions, and I wasn't entirely sure my goody-goody geek-girl reputation was enough to shield me from accusations of skipping class, breaking and entering, and truck theft. I was willing to face up to those things, but I had to cure the zombie virus first. It would be hard to fault someone for skipping AP Bio and committing a few misdemeanors when she had just identified a new disease, right? At least, that was what I hoped.

I expected the locker room to be deserted since it was the middle of sixth period. But when I pushed the door open, I heard a high-pitched yelp. "She bit me!" I wasted no time; I dashed around the corner and nearly took out Mindi Skibinski.

"Ohmygod," she gushed breathlessly. "Kate, you are *just* the person we need. There is *something* wrong with Kiki, and I do *not* know what to do." She jiggled her head at me to emphasize her words.

I eased the door closed behind me. "What happened? Someone

bit you?" The thought of something happening to Kiki made my heart race.

"Yeah!" Mindi held up a hand. I didn't see anything but a little red semicircle near the meat of her thumb. No blood. I felt like telling her this was nothing compared to the chunk Jonah took out of my leg, but she was close to tears already. Besides, I was trying to inspire confidence, not make her doubt my sanity.

I tried to stay calm. "Where is Kiki now?"

"Back here. I think she's got the *flu* or something, and we were all getting ready for the introduction of the homecoming court at the assembly, because of course we *need* to look our best, but she's this nasty green color that totally *clashes* with her dress, not like anyone cares because she's still a *nice* person, and—"

I walked toward the bank of toilets, where a few girls in formals clustered around a closed stall. They parted as I approached; I opened my tote bag with a flourish and produced a syringe. They oohed appreciatively, although that might have been in my head.

"Everything will be fine," I said, holding a hand up in what I imagined was a calming manner. "Just let me through."

I knocked lightly on the stall door. "Kiki?" I said. "It's me. Kate. Can I come in?"

"Yeah," she replied, unlocking the door.

I didn't waste any time. I sprang into the stall and stabbed the needle into the first bit of flesh I saw. It sank in right under her collarbone, which wasn't the best choice in the world locationwise, but it was only my second zombie combat, so I felt a little justified in being hasty.

"Ouch!" Kiki yelped, clapping a hand to her shoulder. "What the heck?"

I stepped back and waited for the vomit that seemed to follow the cure. I didn't want to get any on me. I would have liked to give Kiki a bib or something, because she was probably going to ruin her formal, but I didn't happen to have one. I didn't have a dress either. I made a mental note to go shopping tomorrow. For a moment I wondered what Aaron's favorite color was, but then I shook myself back to the present. The stupid dress didn't matter. If we all managed to make it, I'd wear my Easter dress from when I was thirteen, because who was really going to care what I was wearing? Sadly, I was so underdeveloped that it would probably still fit.

Kiki still hadn't puked. She was too busy staring at me in an accusatory manner.

"Kate, are you crazy?" she asked.

"Um . . ." I blinked. "You aren't feeling sick? Mindi said you bit her."

She laughed deprecatingly. "Yeah, I did. I was just kidding, though. I'm a little nervous about the whole homecoming queen thing, you know?"

"Nervous enough to bite somebody?"

"I guess." She called out the bathroom door. "Sorry, Mindi! I'm just a total nervous wreck. You can bite me back if you want to!"

"You *wish*!" Mindi said, and everyone laughed except me. I was too busy trying to figure out whether I'd just cured Kiki or not, and how I planned to justify my actions since she obviously didn't realize she was a zombie in training. Maybe they only puked if it was a more advanced case? I was beginning to wish there was a zombie combat manual. I could have used one.

"Did . . ." I didn't know how to ask this, so I just plunged right in. "Did Logan kiss you or anything? Like, um, bite you?"

She cocked her head, giving me a considering look. Then she said, "Can we have some privacy, girls?" Before I could ask what she was doing, she reached around me and closed the stall door.

"All right," she said, "you better tell me what's going on before I flip out on you. I'm willing to give you the benefit of the doubt, but that whole injection thing? So not cool."

"I'm sorry. The injection won't hurt you; it's not like a hallucinogen or anything. I thought Logan . . . I thought he infected you with, um, something."

"He's got an STD?" Her eyes widened. I knew I had to correct her, because Logan was a nice guy and I didn't want to damage his reputation, but I couldn't decide whether it was worse to be STD Guy or Undead Guy.

"I don't think so," I said. "A lot of things can be transmitted by saliva. But what I gave you won't hurt you. I just . . . I was worried. There's a bug going around the team."

"Well, I guess I don't blame you, although it would have been nice if you'd asked first." She hugged me and I was so relieved that I hugged back. "So I heard you're going to homecoming with

Aaron, right?" She sounded like she was teasing, but I suddenly felt nervous. What if she still liked him? What if I was breaking the friend code? "It's okay," she went on. "You'll be awesome together, and I really mean that. Aaron and I are much better as friends."

"Oh. Good," I said, opening the stall door. "Because I wouldn't want things to be weird, you know?"

And then someone screamed.

CHAPTER
twenty-one

I could tell the difference between an immature-freshman-type scream and a zombies-are-chasing-me scream, and I immediately knew this was the former. But still? My hand instinctively went to my bag.

"See you in a few," said Kiki, totally ignoring the ruckus. "I've got to finish my makeup."

I walked into the hallway. *Pffft!* "Pep rallyyyyyyyyyyy!" shouted some random idiot, spraying Silly String at my face. He missed, but I was still angry on principle. I bet people wouldn't do things like that if they knew I was the only thing standing between them and zombiedom. Unfortunately, I couldn't exactly publicize this unless I felt like starting a mass panic. Which I didn't.

Rocky walked up and smacked the guy on the back of the head, wiping the smile right off his face. I didn't know how she got away with things like that, but I assumed it must have something to do with the whole cute thing she had going on. He turned around to yell at her, but then his teenage-male brain registered her hotness. That was the end of the altercation right there. It was almost enough to make me contemplate a makeover.

One of his friends jerked him down the hall; he gave Rocky one last longing glance before he finally left us alone. She rolled her eyes.

"Hey, Rocky. Did you bring your phone?"

"Got it." She patted her pocket. "What am I filming?"

I pulled her back into the locker room, picked a corner where the homecoming court wouldn't overhear, and briefed her on the new developments. I edited some of the gorier details, though, because it seemed only kind.

"All right," she said, "so you're going to run around stabbing people with syringes? Because I'm not sure that'll go over well."

"I hope I don't have to do anything. I'm hoping nothing will happen until the health department looks at my data and sends in their zombie-preparedness posse. Assuming, of course, that they don't decide I'm a crackpot."

"So we're the backup plan?"

I nodded.

"Got it," she said. "What do I do?"

"Stick with me. If there's any zombie action, record it. And stay back so you don't get infected too, okay?"

"Roger, Captain."

She mock-saluted, and I had to smile a little. She still didn't quite believe me. But I knew she'd be safe, and I'd have video evidence to back up everything else I'd left for the health department. Because otherwise, I worried that they might not believe me.

Might not? Ha. No way they'd believe me.

I figured the gym would be full by this time, allowing us to slip into the crowd unnoticed. My teachers had better things to do than scan the stands to see if I showed up, but I didn't need to be cocky either. We stopped to say goodbye to Kiki. She looked even more gorgeous than usual.

"You look hot," Rocky said, snapping a picture.

"Good luck!" I said, as if my positive karma extended to things like the homecoming court. Kiki beamed anyway.

Rocky and I slipped into the flow of people streaming down the hall toward the gym and staked out the very end of the bleachers near the doors. The location was ideal; I'd be able to intervene quickly in a crisis. It was impeccable planning, except for the part where we accidentally sat in the burnout section. For some reason, the burnouts didn't like that. The guy next to me had so many piercings that the scent of metal hung in the air around him. I smiled weakly and moved over to give him more room. Actually, I scooted so far that I lost my balance and nearly fell off the bleachers. Coordinated I wasn't.

Principal Wasserman started in on the homecoming speech, which pretty much amounted to "Blah blah spirit blah blah

community blah blah I hope we actually win a game for once."
Well, he didn't say that last part, but I knew he was thinking it.
Everyone was thinking it, except me; I knew it wasn't going to happen, because our team was short a few fingers, half a scalp, and lord
knew what else.

Mr. Wasserman wrapped up the speech and introduced Aaron,
who was looking überhot today. Somehow he managed to find my
eyes in the sea of people. He winked, and I practically dissolved
into a pile of lovesick drool.

"Coach Brzeszczak is out sick today," Aaron said. I was just
impressed that he could pronounce the name without stammering. "So it's my pleasure to introduce the team. We may not always
win, but we leave our hearts out there on the field." I winced at
the unfortunate phrasing. I should have briefed him on the zombie thing, but I'd been too busy running around in circles. "We
work really hard, and I hope you'll come out to support us at Fri-
day night's game. So without further ado, I give you the Bayview
Bantams!"

The marching band burst into our fight song, and everyone
except the burnouts jumped to their feet and started cheering.

A pair of cheerleaders maneuvered a big banner printed with
completely false sayings like BAYVIEW = #1! and BANTAMS ROCK! onto
the floor. I wasn't sure who decided that running through paper
was a great way to inspire pep, but we did this every assembly during the football season. And for some reason, we still lost.

So the band played, and the cheerleaders jiggled, and the pep was positively bursting out of every pore in my body when a player burst through the sign, all by himself.

He was wearing his helmet backwards.

The idiocy was mind-boggling. He waggled his head around, the helmet rocking precariously from side to side. Laughter spread through the crowd. The rest of the players sprinted into the gym, running into Backwards Helmet Guy and sending him staggering. He pawed at the helmet, trying to set it right. It didn't take a rocket scientist to notice he was missing a middle finger.

"Start recording!" I said, but Rocky didn't hear me. So I elbowed her. She stopped midlaugh, looking at me with an offended expression.

"What?"

"Record this!"

I waited until she picked up her phone, and then I dropped off the edge of the bleachers. I wasn't supposed to be down here. It was funny, because I'd broken a lot of laws today, but for some reason, standing under the bleachers during an assembly made me feel like a real rebel.

I marched forward, figuring I could claim student trainer rights and offer to take Mike back to the locker room. But when I stepped out from underneath the bleachers, someone grabbed me by the wrist.

"You're not supposed to be down there," said a familiar voice.

I wrenched my hand away from Swannie, and she laughed.

"Sorry," she said. "I didn't realize it was you."

She winked like we were in on something together. Like she was willing to forget that I'd gotten off the bleachers during an assembly in exchange for my forgetting that she'd infected a bunch of my classmates with a deadly disease.

After seeing what had happened to Mike's mom, I couldn't keep up the charade. "Back off. I'm ending this."

"We had a deal," she said. "You're implicated in this too, remember?"

"I don't care. Are you going to try to stop me?"

"Listen to me," she said, getting right up in my face and speaking low so no one would hear. "If you cross me, I will ruin you. I will swear on a stack of Bibles that you did it all. Hank will back me up. You had access to my lab, my computer, all of it. You won't get into a good school; heck, you'll be lucky if you don't go to jail. All you need to do is shut up and help me fix this, and I'll give you everything you want. A good school. Standing in the scientific community. You should be thanking me."

"Quit trying to bribe me," I hissed. And then, right there in front of the entire student body, I shoved Swannie. Hard.

She flew backward, pinwheeling her arms for balance. Mike staggered blindly in her direction, the helmet still covering his eyes. I could see the collision coming but couldn't stop it from happening. She whirled around and pointed a finger at me.

"It was all her!" she shouted.

Mike blundered into her.

If he hadn't been infected with the zombie virus, he would have just shrugged it off, but now his balance was shot. He staggered. The helmet tilted to the side and toppled to the floor. There was a moment of complete silence while everyone stared at his flip-top scalp and masklike skin. And then the room exploded into chaos.

I was swept away in the flood of bodies. A girl I vaguely recognized from Key Club pushed me so hard that I smacked my chin on some guy's shoulder. Someone shoved me from behind. I went down on one knee. No one could see me; I got whacked in the head, the shoulder, and the head again. I went to all fours, pushing against the press of bodies, trying not to be trampled. A pointy heel pierced the back of my hand, and I howled, but no one heard me.

Aaron appeared in front of me like a vision from God. He hauled me to my feet, shielding me with his torso.

"Are you okay?" he shouted in my ear.

"Where's Mike?" I looked around frantically but wasn't tall enough to see over the crowd. "We've got to find him before he kills somebody."

"What?"

"He's infected with the zombie virus. I can cure him; just get me to him."

Aaron pulled me close. For a second, I thought he was going to kiss me, and while that would have been awfully nice, it wasn't the best timing. But then he wrapped his arms around my waist and lifted me just high enough to look around.

We stood in the middle of a throng of students, all bottle-necked in front of the gym doors. Only one was open; I could see one of the girls from Quiz Bowl mashed up against the other door, struggling to breathe. I looked the other way. There, in the middle of a wide-open expanse of floor, was Mike. He had Swannie by the arm.

I was tempted to let him have her. It was the absolute definition of poetic justice. He pulled her hand closer to his mouth despite her panicked struggles.

Then Aaron let me slide along his body down to the ground.

"That way!" I pointed. "Clear a path for me. I'll deal with Mike."

He looked uncertain. "Deal with him how?"

I pointed to my backpack like that was going to answer his question. To Aaron's credit, he nodded and squeezed my hand.

"Okay," he said. "Be careful."

He released me and dropped into a crouch. "Get out of the way!" he bellowed. Then all the coiled strength in his legs released at once, and he blasted forward, catching the state wrestling champion square in the chest and knocking him to the floor. I'd seen Aaron in quarterback mode before, obviously, but now I realized we'd actually have a chance of winning if he was a linebacker. He was awfully good.

Mike had pinned Swannie's arms to her sides with a bear hug, and he started gnawing on her shoulder. She screamed, but the noise was lost in the uproar.

"Aaron, grab Swannie!" I ordered.

Mike didn't even see us coming, but Swannie did. The panic in her eyes turned to a wild, elated hope as we crossed the last few feet. Aaron wrenched her out of Mike's arms; her flesh came free with a rip loud enough for me to hear. And considering how loud it was in the gym, that was saying a lot. She clapped her hand over the spurting bite mark on her shoulder. The banner-holding cheerleaders couldn't handle it; one fainted dead away. The other puked.

I lunged at Mike with the needle held high. The ideal place to administer the injection was in the thigh or the butt, but there was no way I was going to pull his pants down. Frankly, the idea gave me nightmares. So instead, I went for the easy stick, right on the outside of the arm.

He didn't even seem to feel it when I pushed the needle through his jersey and into his skin. I pressed the plunger. He turned to look at me with an expression of puzzled incomprehension. Over his shoulder, I saw Aaron release Swannie; he didn't know this whole thing was her fault. I put my hands on either side of Mike's head, being careful not to touch the loose flap of scalp, and turned him in Swannie's direction before she could get away.

He puked right in her face. And then she puked on him. Aaron started making his prepuke sound, which I recognized from Coach's office. I had to distract him before this whole situation disintegrated into a total pukearama.

"Get her!" I said, pointing to Swannie. "She's the one who turned him into a zombie."

He did. Then someone tapped my shoulder; I spun around fully expecting to see Principal Wasserman or someone else official, but it was Jonah's friend Drew.

"Dude, do you need some help?" he asked. "I've got a shotgun at home."

"What?"

"A shotgun," Drew repeated patiently. "You've got to destroy the brains if you want to take down a zombie."

"Yeah," said an equally pimply flunky at his side. "A sledge-hammer would do if you don't know how to shoot."

"These are your classmates, you idiots." I wanted to shake them.

Then someone else tugged on my sleeve. It was Principal Wasserman. He looked so scared I thought he might pee. "You probably want an explanation for all this, don't you?" I said.

"No." He shook his head, pointing down at my feet. "But if you don't do something, I think he's going to die."

I looked down. It was Mike. He looked dead again.

But this time it might have been for real.

CHAPTER twenty-two

I felt an intense wave of déjà vu as I knelt by Mike's prone body with Aaron by my side. Principal Wasserman was holding Swannie firmly by the arm; he nodded at me as if to say it was all taken care of. I could concentrate on Mike.

Mike's systems had started functioning normally again, and that included his circulatory system. He had taken a lot of damage while he was infected, and now his wounds were gushing. Making up for lost time, maybe.

I flipped his scalp closed and looked around for something to wrap it with. Aaron whipped his shirt over his head and held it out to me. I ripped the fabric into long pieces, wrapping them around Mike's skull and tying them in place. In my peripheral vision, I could see some of my classmates ease progressively closer as curiosity won out over fear. Now that Mike was cured, they were relatively calm. I couldn't wait to tell them he wasn't the only one infected.

I needed a little nursing backup.

"Where's Mrs. Rooney?" I asked.

"She already left for the day," said Principal Wasserman. He inched forward to get a closer look.

"Stay out of my light!" I snapped, wrapping the final bandage and tying it with a neat knot. "And I need another shirt."

The air filled with flying clothing. One shirt smacked against the side of my head, the sleeve wrapping around my neck. I heard a "Sorry!" from somewhere in the crowd but didn't bother to acknowledge it. The blood from Mike's wounds was soaking through; I couldn't keep up.

"You rip." I thrust a handful of shirts at Aaron and he tore into them, piling up a small mountain of bandages before I even managed to tie another one in place. I worked frantically, my neck dripping with sweat. Wisps of hair escaped from my braid; one plastered itself to the corner of my mouth, but I didn't dare pause long enough to wipe it away.

"Tell me how to take care of the finger," said Aaron. "I can handle it if you'll tell me what to do."

I spared a moment to glance at him, because this was his best friend, after all. I knew I'd freak if Rocky was bleeding out on the floor. He looked pale but focused. I figured if he was willing to put his trust in me, he deserved the same courtesy in return.

"All right." I nodded, grabbing a strip of fabric and beginning to wrap it around Mike's scalp. "First, examine the finger. Is there enough of a nub? Enough to wrap?"

A pause. "No. No nub."

"Okay. Then you're going to wrap in a figure eight. Around the wrist, cross over the missing digit, and back around the wrist again in the opposite direction. You're going to need a lot of layers, and they need to be as tight as you can make them. Tie them off with square knots, nothing fancy. Can you do that?"

"Yeah. Probably not as pretty as you can, but I'll manage."

"Thanks." I attempted to brush the hair out of my eyes with an elbow, even though I knew it was a physical impossibility. I was so tired. "Has anyone called nine-one-one?"

"They're on their way," Principal Wasserman said. "Just a few minutes more, Kate."

By this time, Mike's head was swathed in a huge multicolored turban. I paused and eyed it critically, but nothing was seeping out. I checked his pulse; it was weak but steady, and his respiration was good. I was afraid to say so out loud, but I thought he was going to be okay. Aaron carefully wound another strip over the severed finger. I could only see a small spot of blood there, so that was good. I didn't know what shape Mike would be in when he woke up, but he seemed stable for the moment.

"Keep an eye on him, will you, Aaron?" I asked.

"I'm on it."

I stood up and had a moment of peace before the questions

started flying. My classmates were scared and on the verge of revolt. They surged forward. I couldn't even figure out who was talking; my eyes darted from side to side and saw nothing but panicked expressions and barely restrained hysteria.

"Where did the zombies come from?" asked someone on my left.

"Are there more of them?" said another.

"Are these Romero slow zombies, or *28 Days Later* fast zombies?"

"They were totally slow, dude. Are you blind?"

"Who are you calling blind?"

"Stop!" I shouted, and the silence was instantaneous. I'd never had this kind of power over a crowd, except maybe when I was in grade school and the teacher used to leave me in charge of the class when she had to go to the bathroom.

"Okay. There's no reason to panic." I used my most businesslike voice, speaking loudly to carry to the back of the crowd. "It's true that there's a virus on the loose, but I've got a cure. Everything is under control."

"Is it contagious?" Rocky asked, pushing her way to the front of the crowd.

"Yes."

"How do you know if someone's infected?"

"Well, there are a lot of signs, but the biggest thing to look for is black vomit."

"Oh my god," said a guy from the back of the crowd. "I puked this morning."

"So did I," said someone else.

The crowd scattered, fleeing for the doors again. Even Principal Wasserman disappeared this time. I could only hope he had Swannie with him.

A small group of people was moving against the stream of traffic in my direction—five or six guys, including Jonah's friend Drew.

I heard Drew say, "That one's limping. He must be one of them. Get him!"

Five pieces of plastic pipe rose over the crowd in unison. I recognized them immediately, as only the older sister of an übernerd can. Pseudoswords. I would have been impressed at the guys' synchronicity if I wasn't so annoyed.

"Stop!" I shouted, jogging over. My shoulder slammed into Drew's ribs; I heard the rush of air as his lungs emptied. He toppled into the rest of the vigilante squad. We fell into a tangled heap of limbs on the floor.

I was lying on top of Drew, which was not a position I wanted to be in. He looked up at me and said, "Hey!" All indignant too, as if I was the one not following orders instead of the other way around.

I snatched his pseudosword and hit him with it. Not hard or anything, and not in the face. More like the kind of smack I gave Armstrong when he chewed on the furniture. Drew looked at me with the same expression as Army, the reproachful but contrite one. It worked better on the dog.

"Are you deaf or just stupid?" I said, pushing myself to my feet.

"What do you mean?" Drew seemed honestly confused, so I guessed the answer was stupid.

"I said I could cure the infected. I cannot, however, cure someone after you've bashed their head in. Got it?"

"Oh." His face fell. "I didn't hear that part. We ran to my locker to get the swords."

"Idiot." I looked down at my leg. A fresh red stain was spreading down the leg of my jeans. It didn't hurt much; I couldn't decide if that was good or bad.

A squad of EMTs rushed into the room, led by Principal Wasserman. He was dragging Swannie by the wrist. She was pale but standing tall. Good. It was nice not to have to worry about them on top of everything else.

"Get out of here," I told Drew. "And don't go hitting anybody. If you see someone you think is infected, call me." I gave him my cell number.

"Okay." He hung his head as he started to trudge away.

"Hey, wait a minute," I said, and he stopped hopefully. "Can I have your sword? I'll get it back to you later."

He looked like he couldn't decide whether to be excited or disappointed, but he handed it over. I shouldered it and started for the doors. "Rocky, keep an eye on the vigilantes here, will you?"

And then my vigilante self walked out into the battle.

CHAPTER
twenty-three

A huge stretch of woods ran along the back of our school. My house was actually on the other side; during my ninth-grade environmentalism kick, I refused to go anywhere in a car and actually walked to school through the woods. It was about a mile and a half if you went by street but only ten minutes if you didn't mind slogging through the mud.

I knew from experience that the woods were always wet, really borderline marshland. And on a gray day like today, they were also dark and spooky.

I walked out the back doors and nearly tripped over a Roman chariot made out of about a half ton of tissue paper. I'd forgotten that the homecoming court was planning to make a big entrance on one of the floats. Kiki leapt off the back of the chariot and ran up to me. She held an umbrella over her head, but the bottom half of her dress was still spattered with rain. The rest of the court huddled under jackets and sheets of plastic. They looked miserable and bedraggled, but I couldn't drum up too much sympathy. I'd told them the float was a stupid idea, but no one ever listens to me.

Kiki grabbed me by the shoulders, nearly whacking me in the face with the umbrella. "Kate! Thank god! Do you have any idea why most of the student body's running around in the woods like idiots? And where's Mike? He's supposed to pull our chariot into the gym."

In the distance, I heard a long and drawn-out scream.

"I don't have time to explain. Take everyone inside. Rocky and Aaron will fill you in." Kiki didn't even pause; she started hustling the girls toward the doors.

"Wait a minute," I called. "Take this. And if anyone wacks out or throws up on you, stab them and press the plunger."

She took the syringe I handed her with the tips of two fingers, like she was afraid if she held it too tight it might explode.

"Kate? This is another needle."

"And I hope you don't have to use it," I replied.

She looked down at it, and I could see the questions in her eyes.

"Please trust me," I said. "I don't want to have to worry about you. Rocky knows everything; she'll explain it all."

Kiki nodded. "Good luck," she said. "Come back safe."

I felt immensely cool as she herded the rest of the girls inside and closed the door behind her. The bolt latched into place with

a loud clunk. I had this intense urge to bang on the door and demand to be let inside, but I couldn't do that.

It was game on, zombies. Game. On.

I tromped into those woods like I owned them, scanning for
flashes of yellow and white. It was a good thing our team had nice
bright uniforms; it made target practice a lot easier. Although that
might have been one of the reasons we never won. Instead of cutesy
bright uniforms, maybe we should have worn all black. And spikes.

Within the first three minutes, I ended up ankle-deep in mud
in a huge hole. I was soaked from head to toe, and the constant
drizzle made it tough to see. My smeary glasses turned everything
into amorphous blobs. One of the blobs reached for me; I whacked
it with my pseudosword and prepared to inject, but it turned out
to be a branch blown by the wind.

I stumbled into a clearing. In the springtime, it was probably
the kind of place you'd like to hang out with sparkly vampires. But
it was slightly less attractive in the rain. The blurry zombies didn't
help much either.

There were probably about twenty of them, although I didn't
exactly have time to conduct a census. I wasn't sure why they were
all congregating here. Maybe it was instinct. Herd mentality. I was
speculating on this when I realized that they were all clustered
around something. It wore a red sweater. Or maybe the red was
something else entirely.

I couldn't help it. I made a sound, just a little one. It was too
horrible to handle; I didn't know how they were going to live with

what they'd done once I cured them. The noise might as well have been a firecracker; every head snapped around to look at me. So much for ninjalike stealth.

They started moving toward me. Some walked normally; others lurched on unsteady limbs. Two fell to the ground en route and started dragging themselves through the mud on their bellies. The odds were stacked against me. But if I left the zombies, they'd continue to feed on my classmates. Right now, I was the only one who could keep that from happening.

I backed away slowly, looking for the right place to make my stand. My hand fumbled for my cell. It was a good thing I had Rocky on speed dial. When she answered, I said, "You'd better send the EMTs into the woods out back. They're about to have a lot of patients."

"Kate, are you—"

"Love you, Rock."

I hung up before I turned into a total sap and started crying on the phone. There was a good chance I'd never talk to her again, but I hoped she'd understand if that happened. I hoped they would all realize that I couldn't run and live with myself later.

I looked to my right. Logan was closing in fast, his hands outstretched. One of his thumbs was broken off at the knuckle. His face didn't even register surprise when I ran toward him instead of away from him.

I stabbed wildly with the syringe, missing the first time but connecting the second. Then the pack was on me. I pulled out another dose and injected the first limb I could get my hands on. The needle scraped bone, setting my teeth on edge, but I was on to the next anyway.

There were so many of them. The constant press of their bodies knocked me to the sludgy ground. They tore into my arms and legs; I batted their searching teeth away from my face again and again. The pain registered dimly, as did the sickening rip as my flesh separated from my body. But it was like I was in a trance, a never-ending cycle of pop-the-cap-off, stab-the-needle-in, press-the-plunger, withdraw-and-toss-aside.

I didn't know how long it lasted. Black flashes of nothingness at the edge of my vision threatened to shut me down. Blood loss, probably. An arm reached for me. I grabbed it, pulled it close, and fumbled for a syringe.

In the distance, I heard Aaron screaming my name. Or maybe I was hallucinating it. Wishful thinking.

The backpack was empty.

Merciful darkness claimed me and everything went black.

CHAPTER twenty-four

I woke up in a dim room, covered with sheets that smelled funny. I knew I wasn't in my room, but I couldn't see anything without my glasses. I reached out, feeling the pull of adhesive bandages along the length of my arm. It was uncomfortable but not painful. I was either in the early throes of zombie infection or totally hopped up on pain meds.

"Here, let me help," said a male voice.

The overhead lights popped on. I happened to be looking straight at them; my corneas felt like they were frying. I turned toward the blurry figure standing by the door.

"You call that help?" I croaked. "Would you like to stab me with an ice pick while you're at it?"

"Sorry."

I would have recognized that sheepish, apologetic tone anywhere.

"Jonah?" I needed my glasses. I flung my arm out wider, knocking something vaguely lamplike to the floor. "Is it really you?"

He giggled. Yep, it was really him. I didn't know any other teenage male who would giggle in public. Or at all.

"Here they are," he said, putting my glasses into my hand. I felt much better once I rammed them onto my face and could see him for real. He was a little pale, maybe, although it could have been from the fluorescents. Hospital-room lighting isn't particularly flattering under any circumstances.

"Are you okay?" I held out my hand to him; he took it without a single smart comment. I decided I was probably dead. It was the only explanation for the hand-holding.

His sleeve pulled back, exposing a raw, red ring around his wrist. I gasped.

"I think I taped myself too well. But otherwise I'm fine." He pushed his sleeve back down. "I got off pretty easy, thanks to you."

"Yeah, well . . . do you know how I got here? How the guys are doing?"

"Aaron could probably tell you better; he's the one who found you in the woods. He and Dad are both sleeping in the waiting room. They've been here all night."

"All night? How long have I been out?"

"About a day. I finally talked Dad into getting some sleep; I should probably let him know you're up."

I hesitated. "Did—did the cure work?"

"Yep. I got checked out by the health department and everything. They're dosing everyone in town just in case, and they've got all the guys from the woods under observation. You did good."

I lay back, a smile on my lips.

My nurse came in about two minutes after Jonah left. It took a long time to change all the dressings. I polished off a plastic cup of Jell-O while surveying my injuries. I had some potential damage to the tendons in my left ankle and some pretty serious tissue loss on my legs and arms. The nurse patted me on the forehead. "We'll have the plastic surgeon in to see you this afternoon. Don't worry. He'll have you right in no time."

There was no way I could take my chomped-upon limbs to homecoming. Aaron deserved a date who didn't look like the Mummy Queen. I felt like crying.

My cell was on the nightstand. I knew using it was against the rules, but at this point, I didn't really care. Once the nurse left, I picked it up and texted Aaron. *You okay?* I typed. *I'm sorry, but I can't go to homecoming with you.*

The moment I hit send, I instantly regretted it. He didn't respond. Maybe he was relieved at being let off the hook, and he was asking some cheerleader right now. Probably.

But then my door opened and there he was, tired, stubbly, and adorable.

"What do you mean you can't go to homecoming with me?"

"I . . ." I swallowed the lump in my throat and tried again. "Look at me. This is not something you want to be seen in public with, even if I'm allowed to go. I've lost a lot of tissue, and there's a pretty strong chance of infection, and—"

He crossed the space between us with four long strides and kissed me. His arms slid around my shoulders; our lips melded together. My hands tangled in his hair. My heart thumped so loud and so fast I could hear it, which I found really embarrassing. But then I realized it wasn't mine. It was his.

He pulled back all too soon, carefully settling his weight on the edge of the bed.

Then he said, "I'm taking you to homecoming. And if you don't get out of the hospital in time, I'll petition Principal Wasserman to let us use the cafeteria for a night, and we'll put on a homecoming of our own. I said I'd take you, and I'm keeping that promise."

"Yes, but that was before I looked like a chew toy." My voice was wobbly again. When the doctor showed up, I was going to demand to be taken off these meds. They were turning me into a total wuss-girl, and I hated it. If I had a choice between pain and pitifulness, I'd take the pain.

"So?" He shrugged. "I'm attracted to you for your brains and your sense of humor, and . . . you're not really going to make me go all Hallmark here, are you?"

I shook my head.

"Good." He lifted my hand and brushed my knuckles with his lips. "That's settled. Oh, and I'm supposed to tell you that CNN is here. They want to interview you."

It all happened very quickly. My dad gave the okay, and I called Mom to make sure she was okay with it too. Rocky did my hair and makeup. The camera crew set up all kinds of imposing equipment. The reporter showed up at the last minute; I was convinced he was wearing a toupee.

"Rolling in five, four, three, two, one," said the cameraman.

"I'm here with Kate Grable," the reporter said, "high school senior and scientific genius. Thanks to this young lady, the virus that some people say should be named Grable's disease has been stopped short of epidemic proportions, with only two casualties. Memorial services will be held tomorrow for the high school football coach, Hank Brecizizizack—"

"Brzeszczak," I corrected him, hanging my head. Coach was dead. On one hand, he probably deserved it. But on the other? I felt this horrible weight in the pit of my stomach, like I could have saved him if I'd just tried a little harder.

The reporter went on without even pausing. "The other victim has not been identified pending family notification, but officials say she was not infected. Instead, she fell prey to infected and apparently delirious individuals who became exceedingly violent as the disease ran its course. Many people are currently hospitalized in this small Midwestern city, with varying degrees of brain damage due to the disease's devastating effects. Some have gone so far as to call this the zombie virus, because it appears to have spread mainly via bites and has resulted in severe tissue damage and missing digits for many infected. An estimated two hundred people are confirmed to have been incubating the virus, along with approximately forty who had already begun to exhibit symptoms. They owe their lives to this young woman next to me. Kate, how are you feeling today?"

"Um . . . tired? I've been running around a lot lately."

"I imagine." He fixed me with a blazing smile. "Take me through the process. How did you learn about the virus?"

"I'm the student trainer for the football team, and our players were among the first people infected. So I collected some samples, analyzed them, and took the proof to the health department."

"How well do you know Siobhan Swan, the teacher accused of developing what some are calling a weapon of bioterrorism?"

"Bioterrorism?" I shook my head, sitting up straighter. "Not Swannie. Did they catch her? Where is she?"

He consulted a sheet of paper. "According to the official statement, she's in police custody. How does that make you feel?"

"Happy? Sad? I don't know. I'm glad it's over."

"And what is the one thing you're looking forward to the most?"

"Homecoming." I couldn't help but smile. "I've actually got a date this year. Although I have no idea when I'll manage to shop for a dress."

"He sounds like one lucky guy." The reporter turned to the camera. "I'm Thornton Cavalier, reporting to you from Bayview Hospital."

I watched the interview later that afternoon with Rocky and Kiki. The dresses started arriving the next day, completely free, from all over the country. The police posted a guard at my door to keep the reporters from sneaking in, and I had to keep the blinds closed all the time after some twit snapped a picture of me in my hospital gown looking out at the street.

Principal Wasserman sent some flowers with a note that said they were postponing the dance until I was released from the hospital, which I thought was nice. So Rocky helped me try on the dresses. She picked out a wine-colored silk with the kind of low-cut bodice that made me self-conscious even before I tried it on. But it squished my bits in all the right places and actually made me seem like I could in fact be female. The color made my hair look less like fried grass. In this dress, I could go out in public with Aaron and not feel like a complete dork. He might have been interested in me for my brains, but that didn't mean I shouldn't try.

I felt so good in the dress that I actually stood up to give Rocky all the angles. She'd have to be seen in public with me, after all; Aaron and I were planning on doubling with her and Bryan. Bryan had been treated just in case and was officially virus free.

Rocky applauded, and I blushed a little. For once, I didn't hate myself for being such a freaking sap. It was time for me to give myself a break.

I was staring at the mirror when Rocky snapped her fingers in front of my face.

"Hey!" she said. "Are you zoning out on me or what?"

"I was just thinking."

"About what?"

I shrugged. "Aaron was supposed to visit Mike today, see if there's any improvement."

"Yeah." She sighed. "I heard he's still not able to speak."

"Too much brain damage."

"Can we talk about something else?" She held up a box. "Like pick out some shoes or something? It's just so depressing, know what I mean?"

I nodded. And I tried on the shoes, but she could tell something was up. Probably because I sat there with one shoe on for about three minutes.

"Kate," she said. "You're still obsessing."

"I am not!" I folded my arms and stared at her indignantly.

"Then what were you thinking about?"

"I was wondering how I'd diagnose and cure a vampire virus. It never hurts to be prepared."

She groaned. Sure, she was scoffing now, but when the next virus hit, I knew who they'd come to. And I'd be ready.